ECO WOMAN

INITIATION

FANNY BARRY

Blue Heron Book Works, LLC

Allentown, Pennsylvania

www.fannybarry.com
www.blueheronbookworks.com
Blue Heron Book Works
Allentown, PA 18104

To the scientists who consistently awaken the magic of the earth with their passion for discovery.

Contents

Chapter 1...8

Chapter 2...15

Chapter 3...25

Chapter 4...32

Chapter 5...39

Chapter 6...49

Chapter 7...64

Chapter 8...70

Chapter 9...80

Chapter 10...84

Chapter 11...91

Chapter 12...99

Chapter 13...111

Chapter 14...116

Chapter 15...119

Chapter 16...123

Chapter 17...136

Chapter 18...150

Chapter 19...155

Chapter 20...160

Chapter 21...165

Chapter 22...168

Chapter 23...176

Chapter 24...192

Chapter 25 201

Chapter 26 206

Chapter 27 210

Chapter 28 215

Chapter 29 220

Chapter 30 224

Chapter 31 227

ABOUT THE AUTHOR 229

ACKNOWLEDGMENTS

Thanks to my friend, muse, writing coach, and publisher Bathsheba Monk as well as my own personal discipline for helping me keep working despite the inherent obstacles that come our way every day. And thanks to all the people who've fallen back in love with the earth because they've opened their eyes to her beauty. Eyes open, willing to change, we heal her one act at a time.

Chapter 1

"But what about my parents?" Maeve screamed, looking back across the Hudson River to the gray citadel of West point. Red and yellow flares were smoking from inside the compound, obscuring the helicopters that were launching straight up and spinning around like confused mosquitoes before getting their bearings and flying straight to where Maeve and KB struggled to escape up the cliffs. "We've got to go back!"

"Keep your head down and run, will you," KB answered. He slipped while grabbing a seedling, and by force of will pulled himself back on the path. "They see us."

A helicopter with West Point Military Academy insignia on the tail and doors hovered slowly above, obviously looking for the two fugitives and clipping the tree lined ridge that overlooked the Hudson River. Clumps of leaves and debris flew everywhere, swept up by the helicopter blades.

"They're turning into water molecules even as we speak!" Maeve insisted. "We're running out of time."

"For God's sake, Maeve, focus on the problem at hand. We can't save your parents if we're dead. Cloak and run!"

She tried shifting into transparency, hiding her body

from view. But her energy was spilling all over the place. All she could do was jump up and down in place trying to figure out where to channel it. The excitement of having escaped being swept down a giant drain into the Hudson River, just an hour earlier, was amplified by the fact that her parents had been swept into the abyss instead of her. Well, that and the almost unbelievable fact that she reached for KB and pulled him out of the swirling current instead of her father.

"Pretty please, Maeve! I'm begging you," KB said, pulling her along. "We've got to get out of here. I used up a lot of juice back there and I can't keep up. But I'll catch up. Go. Just go."

Maeve frantically weighed her options. She was desperate to go back and save her parents, but KB was the only person who could help her. KB's repertoire of witchcraft included centuries of study while, so far, Maeve's big trip was running around in circles super-fast while doing cartwheels with bags of cement tied to her ankles if she wanted. Her newfound superhero skills weren't yet up to the challenge of reorganizing atoms. And the three sisters, KB's sisters and Maeve's too, who'd coached her and helped her find her way in this new world of magic and power were no longer available. Her near-death battle against the eldest Sadie suggested they'd never be again.

"Your cave?" she asked.

"Yes, go there. Quickly. I'll be right behind you."

She dropped KB's hand, tucked her chin into her chest, and sped along the ridge. She channeled calm and felt her speed pick up until she was going 60 miles an hour along the narrow precipice. It didn't matter if she lost her footing because her feet barely touched the ground. Her energy pooled in her powerful legs and when the *whoop whoop* of the helicopter blades became more and more distant, she dropped onto the plateau, put her head down and grabbed her knees.

"We're okay, KB," she said, breathing heavily. "We lost them." She looked over her shoulder, but he wasn't there. And she didn't see him catching up. "Shit."

The helicopter had honed in on a spot way back on the trail. Mustering her energy, she finally cloaked, diffusing the lines of her body into the landscape and ran back to where the helicopter was hovering, being careful not to give evidence of her presence.

KB was trapped in the middle of the path, clenched fist pumping at the helicopter hovering above him, yelling at them. The helicopter co-pilot threw a rope onto the path near KB, then lowered himself down, grabbing for him.

"KB!" Maeve yelled, "He has a gun!"

KB looked in her direction and realized Maeve was there, her indistinct outline blended with the swirling foliage caused by the rotary wings. He gave her a thumbs up, clenched his eyes and shifted into a badger. But he wasn't strong enough to hold the small furry mammal's shape and slipped back to human form. Back to a badger, teeth bared. Then a human, fist pumping. Again a badger. He couldn't muster the energy to even run away.

Seeing him struggle, Maeve jumped up to grab one of the landing skids. The copter dipped.

"What the hell," the man on the rope yelled to the man in the cockpit as he was swirled around. "Pull up, pull up! Something's got us!"

Maeve hung on to the landing skid, making the copter swerve out of control. The man on the rope climbed into the cockpit, dropping his gun. She swung on the skids like parallel bars, destabilizing the copter until it started making crazy circles. As it came close enough to the ground for her to plant her feet, she held and swung the machine around in circles. Its blades clipped the tops of the trees as she finally let go and sent it barrelling into the sky. She watched it spiral nearly out of control until it gradually regained course and made its way toward West Point. "Probably for reinforcements," Maeve thought out loud and then yelled, "KB! Are you here? Where are you?"

Sweat poured from her forehead and her skin was cold and clammy as she waited for KB to answer. She tried to control her breathing to avoid going into shock. She was sure he was dead.

Suddenly, she started to cry. She was alone and now the only person who could help her find her family was gone. In fact her only remaining family, KB, was probably at the bottom of the ravine she was standing next to. She picked up a piece of tree branch the helicopter had severed from its trunk and gently stroked the bark as she sobbed. "They never think of how they hurt you, do they," she asked the tree and sniffled, despairing. She knew the soldiers would come back soon, this time with back up. She picked up the rifle the soldier had dropped and swung it over her shoulder as she

11

called, "KB!" into the woods.

But her voice only echoed as the trees around her moved in response to the bellow of her call. Had he fallen into the precipice below? She searched over the edge. Had he finally become the badger? Maybe he was too tired to regroup into human form? She looked around for signs of a quickly dug den where he could be hiding. Nothing.

She searched frantically. Who could help her if he was gone? Their mother was a glass of water. Her father? She would never forget the look on his face as he pushed her to her supposed death. It must've been a mistake.

Wasn't it?

But now she would never hear it from him, because KB, the one person who knew how to rescue them, was probably dead. In one horrible day she had lost her entire family. No, she had killed her entire family. Everything that happened was her fault.

"And my destiny?" she sobbed to the tree branch still in her hand. She, who was supposedly meant for great things, couldn't even keep her nearest and dearest safe.
She was full of potential. But only potential. The sudden quiet in the forest around her allowed her to weigh options and she wondered if she would be able to see her parents bodies within the water if she could get close enough. After all, she had incredible eyesight now. Her parents could be slipping away, their molecules dispersing into the constant flow of water toward the sea. Maybe she could go it alone.

She let out a frustrated roar that rumbled through the entire valley, shaking loose rocks on the cliff. The clouds darkened and a crack of electricity lit up the sky right before rain came down, softly at first, then incessantly and Maeve realized she'd better find shelter.

As she moved under the boughs of a pine, a strange fog rose around her feet so slowly she took a while to notice. When she finally did, the moist, gray white cloud had moved to just in front of her face. It then spiraled to form the face of a man, undulating yet totally discernable, like a movie cast onto a sheet in the wind. He was laughing. Wet, dark and curly hair hugged his cheek bones and lower chin. The vision's deep brown eyes smiled into Maeve's and although his mouth didn't move, she heard an echo saying, "You, my dear sister, are destined for great things. Work with me and you will achieve your destiny." The voice paused as the vision came deeper into focus, magically painted on the fog. His face was burnished by sun and a scar above the right eye crossed the side of his face, nearly touching the gold hoop earring sparkling as it trembled slightly on his earlobe. She nearly expected him to recite some pirate phrase like, "Ahrr de arr my darling."

Instead, he whispered hoarsely, "I can teach you what you need to know. I can help you. Find me," the voice eerily continued. "Before I find them," he teased, then burst into laughter and dissipated into the pouring rain, gone in a second.

She rubbed her eyes, not certain if it was a vision or her imagination. She felt her forehead. It was hot. She was delirious. Drops filtered through the tree where she was hiding. She needed better shelter and a plan. Not knowing where else she could be safe, she decided to go to KB's cave. It was around here somewhere, just off this cliff she remembered. She stopped cloaking to save energy.

Too, she reasoned with herself, perhaps if some wildlife could see her, they'd sympathize or at least give her a clue as they ran away. She'd taken only a few steps when she heard the high-pitched growl of an animal in distress. Startled, she stopped in her tracks. Afraid to believe it could be KB, she whispered, "Where are you?" stepping lightly over the wet leaves. She walked down the ledge, kicking up the leaves until she finally came upon a balled up black and white creature; a badger. It was crying. Picking it up, she saw that its foot had been badly smashed and there was a cut on its forehead. A lump was forming behind the bleeding gash. It must have been hit when she was hurling the copter around in circles. "I can't do anything right," she whispered to the wounded creature and held it close to her breast. She began to run just as the whoop whoop of another copter sounded in the distance. "Let's get out of here, KB," she said.

Chapter 2

She clutched the small mammal with the upturned nose to her chest as they ran the ridges south along the Hudson River to KB's chosen exile in Palisades Park. Creating nothing more than a blur on the landscape, they nearly flew through the incredible public acreage of trees and cliffs in the shadow of Manhattan.

Maeve felt the otherworldly vibrations from the nearby labradorite stones as the badger's body went limp against her chest. She hugged him closer, pressing him to her heart, afraid she was losing him. She prayed to her teacher, Kitty, one of the three sisters who saved her life and mentored her into her superhero powers. Maeve doubted they would help her anymore after she almost killed the eldest, Sadie. Still, she felt closest to Kitty, maybe because at only 300 years old, she was the youngest. Kitty was the one who introduced her to the healing powers of the labradorite that formed the cliffs and caves of the Hudson. "They used this type of rock in Stonehenge, England. A mystic healing stone that helps everything from mental clarity to respiratory issues," Kitty had said.

"Help me save him," she called to that northern witch as she leaped over the wall separating the main drive from the ridge. She followed the nearly indiscernible, narrow trail that would take them to KB's abode inside this tall escarpment. Maeve moved boldly, without fear of falling, desperately afraid of losing her brother. The badger hadn't stirred since they started. "C'mon little guy. We're nearly there," she coaxed.

Since her battle at the Old Chapel in West Point – was that really just a few hours ago? It felt like a lifetime – she'd lost her fear of death and barely used the mossy walls of the bluff for support. At one point, she tripped and they fell forward into nothingness, her toes barely clinging to the path. But she held the space, floating for a second before she pulled herself back, leaning into the cliffside and laughing. "We're fine," she consoled the animal who was merely a warm ball of fur in her arms. He didn't react and she almost panicked. How would she ever find her parents without him?

The sound of a helicopter in the distance once again made her pull the wild animal closer and whisper into his ear, "We'll be there any second. Hang on please." When she heard the river rushing more closely she knew that the cave was a quick turn right.

She swung her body into the entry tunnel, instinctively taking the badger in her teeth by the scruff of his neck as she landed on all fours. She growled and turned her head side to side, examining the tunnel, holding her rescued friend like its mother. Once she felt the embrace of the space close around them, she softened her feral demeanor, stood and took him back into her arms. The earth underfoot was soft, the breeze behind her cooled the interior of the Palisades cliffs. She lowered her defenses.

Gently caressing the low, moist ceiling with one hand to keep from bumping her head while holding the wounded animal close with the other, she hurried into KB's expansive cave.

Brusquely pushing rolls of engineering plans off the kitchen table, she gently laid the wounded animal down. It was unconscious. "KB. I know you're in there. Come back. You're safe now," she pleaded.

Nothing.

She passed a hand under its nose to feel for a breath. Again, nothing. "I know you're alive," she nervously challenged the animal. Instinctively she put two fingers on the nostrils of his upturned nose and pried open his jaw. "Let this work," she prayed, as she took her lips around its tiny mouth and exhaled into it, then pressed not too gently on his chest. "Come on," she urged the animal and repeated the sequence 4 more times. "Come on," she called again, ready to scream or cry or both.

Frantic, she lowered her face to wrap her lips around his mouth once again, but he started to quiver and then took a deep inhale. His breath resumed and his dark eyes opened. He rolled onto his belly and lay there, frightened, dark eyes searching for a place to hide, anywhere he could run and burrow into the ground. Maeve extended a hand to touch him but he growled and bared his teeth.

"You can't be serious," she said to the mammal. "I just saved you. Don't growl and take your human form back please. We need to get going." The animal's claws dug into the table as he rested his head between his front legs and

17

watched her warily.

Maeve didn't reach for him again but asked sympathetically, "What's going on? Why won't you come back? It is you, KB, right?" Desperate, she wondered if she'd rescued a real badger rather than her warlock brother. Pacing the space, followed by the beady eyes of the wounded badger on the table, she reviewed what she knew about shape shifting. It wasn't much.

But she remembered Kitty, who slipped in and out of her feral shape as a cat, telling her how it wasn't all that complicated to take a different form. "The form is the illusion. You only need empathy and understanding to enter the shape of another. Well," she had hesitated, "and some magic." Maeve clenched her fists, frustrated that she lacked the last ingredient: magic. Her strength and ability to become invisible couldn't help her bring KB back. She moved closer to the animal who, once again, growled. "C'mon KB. We don't have time for this. What is it? Water?"

She brought a bowl to the table and gingerly pushed it toward him. Warily, as she backed away, the badger crawled over to it and drank. Mesmerized by the lapping of his tongue against the liquid, she realized, "You're weak. Is that it?" She dashed to the fridge. "Wow. The fridge of a man who lives alone. What do you eat, KB?" she mused.

The inside was clean and nearly empty. She grabbed a wrinkled apple from the humidor and cut it into pieces for the obviously hungry animal who had already finished the water. She placed the apple slices on the table and went for more knowing nourishment would give him strength.

"I wish you could talk to me. Tell me what you need 'cause I need you to come back to form. At least your head so you could talk to me." She laughed at a vision of KB's head on a badger's body and watched the animal as he sat back, nibbling the apple pieces she'd left for him.

Maeve looked for signs that the animal was, in fact, KB. "Could I have messed up again?" she asked herself, wondering if she had only rescued a wild animal. The cut on his head had stopped bleeding but you could see the swelling around it, even through the fur. His hind leg was bloody and swelling as well.

"Well, if I'm going to rescue you, I may as well do it right," she told the animal as she looked for a first aid kit but found only gauze, rags and hydrogen peroxide. "I should have known you'd never buy plastic, but band-aids? Couldn't we accept there are situations for non-organic materials?" she asked the badger as he sat on the table, watching her rumble through the drawers and cabinets as he munched the last bits of fruit.

Finally, she took the basic supplies and warily approached the animal. "OK. Let's have a look at those injuries, shall we?" she asked as she reached toward him. He growled, low and menacingly and she pulled her hand back. "Listen, I can't help you if you won't let me. So, if you really are KB, pull yourself together and back off. And if you're not, well get off the table then and heal yourself in the wild."

She prayed she hadn't made another big mistake. She'd already nearly killed two men, beat the crap out of the old woman, Sadie, who'd saved her and taught her pretty much everything about her new life. "And don't forget," her inner critic called, "you've probably killed your parents and now your long-lost brother." She banged her hand on her forehead in frustration and asked herself what Kitty would do.

"Tobacco" came the answer. "Smoke some tobacco," her intuition told her. "I don't smoke," she answered out loud and then heard from an echo in her head, "for the badger, silly. And even if it doesn't work on the badger, a smoke will calm you down, help you think." She nodded to the voice in her head, reminiscing about the times she'd watched her witchy trainers smoke their pipes and talk stories into the night while drying herbs and boiling internal organs from the animals they'd respectfully cooked for dinner.

She found KB's tobacco stash by his bedside. Like his sisters, he too had a small pipe, the bowl in the shape of a cougar's head. She filled it and struck a match to light it, clamping down on the mouthpiece and drawing air through the stem. She coughed as a coil of smoke rose toward the ceiling, then toward the badger, creating a gray bridge of calm. The small animal lifted his nose to breathe it in. Magically they were connected.

Maeve puffed again on the pipe and watched the badger slowly relax on the table. His eyelids drooped and he became obviously calmer.

"Ha, I've found the magic," Maeve congratulated herself and, keeping the pipe going, approached the now sedated animal with the gauze and hydrogen peroxide. "At least I'll cure you before you run off to the wild," she told him as she dabbed the cut on his head with the liquid. "But KB, if you're in there, it's past time to come out. This charade has to stop."

She finished bandaging his foot, toked on the pipe again and scratched the badger behind the ears as he closed his eyes finally and rested. "Well, at least you won't die of infection." She blew a smoke ring toward the ceiling. "Now what?" she asked herself and anyone listening to her prayers. The only sound was the drip of water and the gentle hissing of the pipe as she pulled air through the stem and wracked her brain for ideas on what would stimulate KB's return to human form. She knew it was him now, at least. Any wild animal would run at the smoke, a sure sign of danger from fire. But this little guy was sleeping soundly. He'd welcomed the bandage on his head and foot, as if he knew he needed them.

Snapping back to her need to rescue her parents she scolded him, "I don't have time for this." Impatiently she implored him, "How do I bring you back? Can you tell me?"

The animal snorted in its sleep, and she wanted to scream. Instead, she drew another long drag on the pipe and watched the smoke rings rise to the ceiling. One of them hovered around her to form the shape of a cat, curling its tail around it's legs, before it then turned into a human.

"Kitty!" she exclaimed, excited to have a friend break her loneliness. The image was nebulous and vague but the rhinestone button sparkling at her neck was Kitty's signature.

Maeve reached for the image but it dissipated only to take the shape of a hand that reached for her. Mesmerized, the hand loomed over her forehead and rested there.

Ideas leapt into her mind so quickly she could barely keep up with them until one hovered clearly and the others stopped. Kitty's soft voice recited, and Maeve could see the letters in smoke drifting over her: *coirt an céadar, drúcht na maidine, síoróip mhailpe agus sin é.* She understood the Irish immediately, "bark of cedar, morning dew, maple syrup and that will do." The hand began to dissipate, and the smoke fell away as Kitty's voice became an echo through the space.

She grabbed at the words as they disappeared. She wanted to race toward her old mentor but caught herself, saying, "Slow down." She stared at the badger, still sleeping, unaware of the vision that might turn him back into a human. "Focus," she reminded herself and repeated: "Cedar." Easy, she told herself as she started to exit the cave. She remembered a tree by the entry that would surely donate some bark. But morning had already passed to afternoon and syruping season was well over. She screamed in frustration wondering how to get the simple things she needed.

"Wait," she told herself. "Slow it down. Think," she commanded and turned back into the space to open the freezer in KB's nearly empty fridge. "Sweeeet," she exclaimed as she read out loud, "Pure Maple Syrup, spring 1999," from the label stuck on the mason jar. "Wow, ancient," she chuckled as she pried it from the frozen space. "OK, two out of three," she reminded herself and took a burlap bag from beside the fridge and a small vial with a cork from KB's cabinet. Mumbling to herself she said, "This should do." She paced for only a second, reciting the recipe to herself before she told the still sleeping badger, "Wait here," and then ran from the cave toward the ledge.

Leaping from the tunnel, Maeve once again hovered over nothingness and wondered if she could actually fly before she turned toward where she'd seen the red cedars. She didn't notice how her feet hovered over the ground as she smelled her way toward the soft grove of aromatic pines and scraped a little bark from the tree that appeared the oldest, saying, "Thank-you". She swore the scraggy reddish tree growing over the rocky soil told her, "Happy to help." She glanced back to check but the tree seemed normal. How could everything have become so weird, she wondered.

As she inhaled the delicious fragrance, she wondered, "Kitty didn't recite quantities," and went back to scrape a bit more as she touched the bark and said, "Thank you. I love you," genuinely. It was as if the tree warmed where her hand was and for a second, she was euphoric, connected to its old soul until she remembered the morning dew. "No! I cannot wait until tomorrow morning," she bellowed and let her hand fall to her side before she rushed toward the river, looking into the ferns and small plants that formed by the bank. "Help me," she whispered to the plants, "please," as she searched for a plant that would still have the gentle dew from morning.

She carefully pushed the fronds of ferns aside and even thought about breaking the stems of the jewel weed that she knew was full of liquid. "That's not morning dew," she told herself and she looked for leafy plants where a drop or two might still be waiting for the sun before evaporating. "I will not wait for tomorrow," she called out loud, willing herself to keep looking. "I can't," she whispered to the riverbank and cried, "Please, just a drop or two." Then she looked up toward the sky, closed her eyes and took a deep breath in, recalling the plants that may still hold those precious drops. She fell to her knees and began her search on all fours, leaving a strange imprint on the sandy bank.

As she moved into a soft indent in the bank, just below a gracious root that was holding the earth against the current she found it: Jack in the Pulpit. Almost afraid to look, she knew that this plant might still hold the morning's moisture. Ever so gently, she lifted the hood from the stamen to stroke the inner flower and saw several drops still holding shape within its flower cup. She screamed in glee to see it and noticed there were several of the same delicate flower in this gentle glade. Gratefully, she took the small vial from her pocket and methodically scooped the few drops of this morning's dew from each flower. Holding the container into the light, she whispered to herself, "I hope it's enough," pushed the cork back into it and put it into her bag next to the cedar bark before she turned to nearly fly back to KB's abode.

Chapter 3

Customarily landing on all fours at the entrance, she held the foraged ingredients in her teeth and raced through the tunnel into the cave. She prayed the animal was still there and still alive. Once the space opened around her, she screeched to a stop and stood. The table was empty, a blood-stained apple core lay where the badger had been. At least she had evidence she hadn't dreamt the whole episode.

Plans scattered on the floor bore the footprints of a wounded animal but nothing more. Maeve pulled the bark and vial of morning dew from her mouth, spitting out a few splintery pieces of cedar to lay them on the table. Looking into the dew drops that the vessel guarded she heard Kitty's tinkling voice once again chanting the recipe she hoped would bring her big brother back and let them finally get on track to save her parents. *"Coirt, drúcht, mhínfhuil na mailpe,"* echoed in the cave. She drowned the chanting saying, "I know; Bark, dew, maple's fine blood," and then yelled, "KB? Where'd you run off to?" as she stomped her foot and searched the space. "It's past time to go," she moaned.

She stopped suddenly, noticing the door to the fridge was open. "Did I forget to close the door?" she wondered aloud. But when she opened it wider, she found the wounded badger sitting on the shelf, humidor open, the core of the last apple next to him. A sticky goo ran along its fur and over the edge of the shelf where he was sitting. "My maple syrup!" Maeve yelled angrily, grabbing the gluey jar that lay on its side, open and running slowly toward the floor. The badger grunted, licking its paws as if to say, "My syrup, not yours." Despite all the tension or perhaps because of it, Maeve laughed uncontrollably, holding the door for support.

When she could finally control her hysterics, she reached for the animal only to be greeted by bared teeth and growling. "Starting this again?" she chastised him. "You want to stay a badger?" She looked around for the pipe she'd dropped.

Kitty's vision had given her the recipe to bring him back but she moaned. This whole process was so laborious. She thought magic should be more instantaneous. The wounded animal backed into the far corner of the fridge making it more difficult for her to grab him. Badgers could be fierce when cornered, that much she knew. "Give me a break, would you?" she mumbled as she noticed the pipe's bit protruding from under the plans scattered on the floor. "You've made a righteous mess here," she scolded the animal as she pulled the pipe out, washed it in the sink and stuck it between her teeth as she tapped KB's stash of tobacco into the bowl.

Maeve inhaled a flame into the tobacco-filled bowl and tugged air through the channel as she took three very long draughts. Smoke filled the cave with a comforting smell that was reminiscent of the sisters' northern home. She inhaled patiently on the pipe until the badger's head poked from behind the door of the fridge. She waited as he slowly exited, syrup laden fur clinging to his body as he tiptoed unevenly back onto the plans and finally lay on his belly as if waiting for her to help him.

"So now you're ready?" she asked and blew some smoke over toward him. He calmed down and let his head drop between his paws as she walked toward him, blowing smoke rings that created a halo above his head. They hovered there like a crown for the wounded animal as he closed his eyes and drifted off.

"The miracle of natural medicine," Maeve mumbled as she laid her tools on the table. "Time consuming, but effective. Now what," she asked, wondering how to use them. The bark, she imagined, had to be boiled. But there was so little dew water that she didn't dare to boil it with the bark. "It'll evaporate," she told herself. "So how?"

Maeve walked to the fridge, pipe between her teeth, and pulled the nearly empty syrup container from the shelf. She examined how much she had left and despaired of ever getting this concoction together. "My parents are disintegrating, and you won't materialize to help me," she scolded the sleeping badger. Sitting on the stool by the table, Maeve searched her ingredients for clues, wondering how to combine them all.

Before she could overthink it, she stuck the reddish bark into the syrup container and stirred it into the goey liquid. "I need more," she realized and took a knife to scrape the glutinous residue from the fridge.

"Not bad," she commented as she held the jar in front of her face observing the cedar's red color as it moved into the syrup. She stirred the wood pieces in the viscous liquid once again, letting the pipe protrude from one side of her mouth as she gripped the mouthpiece in her back teeth and started humming. Circles of smoke continued to fill the space and hover over the badger whose alarmingly loud snoring was shaking books from the uppermost shelf in the cave.

Maeve pushed the wood into the now rose-colored mix and noticed it had softened. She worked the bark deeper into the container, creating a pasty, sticky poultice that she hoped would cover the badger's wounds and enter his bloodstream. "That must be it," she mused and chanted, "*chumasc*", over and over as she continued working the now clay-like mixture. She began humming the Beatles' song, "Come Together" and, satisfied that she'd massaged it enough, she opened the vial and let the dew drops slowly fall into the mix. "So little," she whispered, praying it would work as, for a second, the droplets simply rested there, cohesive tension keeping them from absorbing into the mix. Hopeful within the realm of pure elemental theory, Maeve wondered if her parents would be able to use that same force to stay separate within their liquid prison. But then the bond broke and the droplets sank into the mixture. As they did, a faint steam hissed to the surface smelling deliciously of maple and cedar bark.

Maeve ran to the comatose animal and lathered the mix onto his head and injured foot. She instinctively rubbed it behind his ears and let her two index fingers draw the sweet earthen mixture down the line of his spine, finishing just shy of his tail. She repeated that motion, back of ears to tail, three times and then stood back, scraped the last of the mixture from the jar and rubbed it under his chin.

Nothing happened.

Dismayed, she licked the edge of the jar to taste the mixture. "Not bad. But come on. I'm not baking cookies here. Can you do something?" she coaxed the wild animal searching for some shift, some change in his identity.

Again, nothing.

She toked on the pipe in a frustrated nervousness. "*Tá tú ag teastáil uaim*, KB, I need you," she nearly cried.

Slowly, the white and black fur faded from exactly where she had rubbed the mixture down his spine to show only skin. As an incoming tide slowly moves over sand, the badger's hair sank into itself, and its fur subsided to show naked skin. Maeve's eyes opened wider as she watched the transition. She took the pipe from her mouth as she witnessed the nose shrinking and flattening. The body began to inflate and extend as the claws receded into finger and toe nails. Legs and arms painfully lengthened as the shape grew and the skull made popping sounds as it reformed into that of a human. The facial fur turned into a beard and in a minute's time, a naked, shivering man sat up, eyes wide as if not recognizing the place or Maeve. He turned his head side to side and then stretched his arms overhead creating more pops from his newly expanded joints until he smiled and told her, "That feels so good."

29

"Ha!" she laughed and blew a smoke ring towards him. "It worked. It worked! I thought I'd lost you." Tears of relief and happiness ran down her face as she teased and handed him a robe, "A badger, KB? Seriously? Not very ferocious. Your tendency toward the underground is disturbing."

He was preoccupied with examining his wounds and moving his fingers, toes and spine. His foot was swollen but he raised the gauze padding she'd put on it and saw it was a clean slice. "I'm glad they didn't sever it with that blade," he told her. "I'd have to shift into an iguana then to grow a new one."

She laughed, "Neither choice is very intimidating." Overjoyed, she poured more antiseptic into the cut.

"Jeez, not so much. That stings like crazy." He pushed her hand with the bottle away and gritted his teeth, "Let me take care of it from here will you? I've healed from more devastating injuries."

"Suit yourself," Maeve said, hurt.

KB grabbed her wrist as she turned away, "It's not that I'm ungrateful. I appreciate you saving me. But I know what I need to do to heal this. And it was actually the blow to the head that put me out. Honestly, I've been through worse."

"Well, heal it then," she demanded. Overwhelmed once again by the instinct to run and find her parents she reminded him, "We don't have much time."

KB kept her hand in his. He didn't know if he even had the strength to plan Maeve's parent's recomposition, let alone do it. "I'm getting there," he assured her, "We'll be on the road soon with the knowhow to get them back into shape, literally."

Chapter 4

Ideally, he'd stay in the cave and rest for a week or more, letting his body heal. And that was in his younger days. Like his sisters, his recuperation time had grown as he'd aged. And the last few days had been draining, emotionally and physically. To heal the wounds faster would be even more so.

Maeve sensed his doubt and saw the exhaustion in his face. She was concluding that she'd have to go it alone. She could, she knew. But the thought intimidated her. She coached herself, trying to build confidence while she watched KB limp around the cave and exercise his foot in ways she found archaic. He'd try some jumping jacks and then lay on the floor with his feet to the ceiling, circling his ankles. "Where'd you learn that physical therapy?" she called to him. He ignored her and jumped back to his feet to do some pushups but fell to his belly and rested there. "I think you could do with more of that bark and dew. Maybe all of you didn't come back," she called to him.

"I'm all here, don't worry," he assured her. "Not everything is a quick spell. I need to recover and movement helps. Trust me."

She didn't and preferred to believe that he could and should magically get himself going. After all, magic wasn't so hard: listen to your inner voice and practice patience and faith. That seemed to be the bottom line. The patience thing was challenging her right now but she had to admit, if these exercises worked, it would be magic.

And she'd need magic to help her parents. After all, calming an injured warlock trapped inside a wounded animal was amazing. But it was still a far cry from recognizing and reorganizing human form within water molecules. And if she messed it up? Her parents could come back mutilated. Images of her mom with a head coming out her ear and her dad with an arm for a nose filtered through her mind. Worse, she could mix their body parts and bring them back joined to each other. Her mother would be furious. Her father? Perhaps he deserved it for trying to send her into the void. Frustrated, she stomped her foot on the ground, shaking the entire space as she finally let go and sobbed. KB wasn't the only one who needed a week to recuperate in the cave. Maeve was on edge.

Taken aback by her raw emotion, he suggested, "Hey, sit down. Inhale and absorb the vibrations. These stones are healing." The vaulted ceiling shimmered with the cool stones. But the comfort they emitted felt wrong. He let her sob, realizing she needed to let it go as he fingered the lump on his head. "Living with these minerals has cured me in many ways. You'll feel better here. You'll see."

"But we can't stay long," she said through sniffs, trying unsuccessfully to control her outburst. "Only long enough for you to heal and make a plan." KB stopped his exercising to slowly undo the gauze she'd wrapped around his nearly crushed foot. She absentmindedly examined the swollen member with him. "These toes look like dumplings for God's sake. Grab me some ice, will you?"

Calling over her shoulder as she pulled two ice packs from the fridge she confided, "I need to know why my father

33

would ever want me gone." She vividly remembered her father calling the cascading water to wash her away and shivered at the realization that her father might have an agenda that wasn't in her best interest. The idea confused her. Could he actually want her out of the picture? Wasn't she his special girl, his amazing protege? She'd worked so hard for his approval and trusted he always had her back. That he might not care about her well-being or, even worse, that he might be working against her now cut her deeply.

No gauze or bandage could heal that emotional wound. She distractedly placed one ice pack on the bottom of KB's foot and another on top. She commented, "It might work better to put your foot in a bucket filled with ice water."

Withstanding the cold of the ice packs, KB answered, "Thanks for thinking of a more torturous way to heal."

"It'd be faster."

"I'm a quick healer. Don't worry."

But he was worried. His foot and head throbbed as he reviewed chemical formulas in his mind that might, and it was only might, bring her parents back. He would focus on their mother. Little by little, Maeve would realize her father was no longer on her side, their side. Even KB couldn't believe Victor was willing to let his little girl wash away. "So disappointing," he thought of the narcissism that ran so deep he would sacrifice his own. But then, KB smugly remembered how rats send their young to forage and risk death at the hands of predators to preserve the hierarchy.

Maeve interrupted his reverie. "I mean if you'd shifted into a deer you could have run out of there. A badger? Where did that come from?"

"Shape shifting in an extreme situation isn't always planned out thoughtfully," he defended himself, moving an ice pack to his forehead. "Regardless, badgers can dig quickly into the earth and cover their burrows to protect themselves. With the soldiers after us, I only thought of protection. It's a good example of what might happen if we run to get your parents without a decent plan. It can all go wrong in a second."

He put his hands over the ice packs and started to chant. *Tabhair dom an solas, slánaigh mé ón troid seo*, "bring the light, heal me from this fight," he repeated and swayed side to side.

Maeve watched him chant his healing mantras, waiting for him to snap out of it and be done but then reminded herself, "patience and faith." She wandered the cave as his chants echoed off the stones and remembered healing on a cot in the corner when KB and Kitty had nursed her back to health from her near death experience at the PCB plant. Kitty mixing clays to extract the PCB toxins in the simple kitchen on one side while KB researched what mixes would work best in the office space on a stone outcropping opposite.

Lost in her reverie, she stubbed her toe on something in a far corner.

"Ouch!" She jumped up and down rubbing her toe then examined the offending large urn-like container. It

35

caught drops of water running down the stones on the side wall, "from the source." Kitty's melodic voice echoed in the gentle rhythm of the drips as they entered the vessel that fed an oversized aquarium built along the length of the floor. There were small fish darting through the edges and the bottom gradually rose to support what looked like a mini mangrove swamp.

Fascinated by the construction, she kneeled next to it to get a better look and immediately, the small engine at the far end sprang to life to send a wave rippling over the waters. Fish darted into the area around the roots of the mini trees as the waves approached. When they hit the micro swamp, they dissipated and the doll sized shack KB had placed at the far end, only received a gentle kiss from the would be tsunami. The drips, the bubble of the filter, water rushing through a few circular tubes and now the gentle lapping of the waves blended with the shuffle of papers from KB's searching.

KB was walking, nearly healed. He grabbed a set of plans and used them to point toward the model saying, "That's one of my favorite demos. I use it with community groups to demonstrate how valuable our coastal dunes and marshes are. Bummer is that people forget as soon as they want to have a condo that overlooks the sea and the only place to put it is smack dab in the middle of coastal protection."

Ready to go she confided in him, "I hardly noticed all the details the last time I was here."

"In and out of consciousness you wouldn't. Have a

seat over there," he directed her to the space on the carpet, balancing on his uninjured foot while circling the other.

"This place will calm your nerves and relax you. Take a good look around 'cause not many people know this place."

"KB, how would they? You live in a cave," she reminded him.

"I suppose that might have something to do with it," he laughed, still getting used to the pushback. "People exhaust me. I like the inaccessibility. And with these stones I can block the sisters and even the council. I never liked being monitored."

Maeve sat on the carpet cross legged and caressed the pile, letting the warm wool run through her fingers and palms. Suddenly, she nearly shouted, "What am I doing here with you? We should be on our way to find my parents. You're nearly ready."

Sympathetically he told her, "Nearly. But I'm still healing and we need a plan, remember? We'll get one shot at this and we need to know exactly what we're doing. You think closing Sadie's factory was an impromptu idea? That was months of planning and research. Stop focusing on movement and use your mind." He was the exasperated one now.

Maeve was all too aware that her newfound gifts seemed to be more physical than intellectual, but she didn't know how to improve that side of her power without asking the three sisters. "Well," Maeve reminded him, "We don't have months, KB. And I can't wait another day." She paused as he continued playing with his exercises. "I've been thinking of asking the sisters for help." The word "sisters" echoed off the stones. "Kitty's been contacting me visually. She's the one who gave me the recipe for your foot, you know? She'd help with spells to reconstruct my parents. And she'll know where they are for sure. If you're not ready, I still need to go. I can't wait longer. I hope you understand."

She turned to get her backpack but he caught her arm. "Let me show you something." He threw plans on the floor and limped over to the archaic television, moving the antenna slightly to the left and adjusting the knobs. Holding her hand to keep her from leaving, he closed his eyes and chanted, *taispeáin dom an fhírinne*, several times in a low whisper. She'd enjoyed hearing the melodic Irish and now was never surprised when she used or understood it. "Show me the truth," she repeated the English as she impatiently waited and remembered how she'd found her heritage with the sister's in the north. She was ready to go back there any second until the room's soft glow was interrupted by flashes of the screen flickering to life. She put her pack on the floor and KB opened his eyes slowly, still in trance and then smiled, adjusted the knobs again and said, "Voila. Our portal opens. We're connected to the shadow source.

Chapter 5

He sat close to the machine and motioned to Maeve to sit with him, patting the carpet at his side. She conceded, "OK. I'll wait but this needs to be substantive or I'm heading north for help." Yet she loved sitting next to him, like the siblings they were, two kids vying for closeness to the screen. She felt the closeness she was looking for. It was like being home. In fact, the way he put his arm over her shoulder was just the way her dad would.

She hoped he had a good plan because she wanted to work with him as he casually explained, "You'll understand more after this. Trust me, your parents are ok. And I'm still not 100% sure how I do it but here's the Shadow channel. I've tapped in using old technology and my own clairvoyance to transmit what they're doing. So far, it seems, they have no idea."

Under the dome of the cave, Maeve heard the ocean roar as she leaned into the TV and watched men hustling, shouting, moving lines and attaching weights and anchors to fish pens they lowered into the water. They were far out in the ocean, no land in sight. The water's deep greenness told her it was not a tropical location. She watched the hooded heads of divers come to the surface like seals and descend again, investigating underwater. "Where is this?" she asked, watching the television's incredibly clear color picture, nearly feeling the motion of the ship as it and its crew were thrown about by rough seas and wind.

The picture shifted to one man on deck holding his balance, legs spread wide, feet firmly planted. She inhaled, recognizing the rugged face and distinctly dark energy. It was the same face that had risen from the fog after they left West Point. She'd never forget it. Still unsure whether to share her vision with KB she nonetheless backed slightly away from the set and commented, "He's Shadow, obviously. Rough and handsome in that rugged sort of way, like a pirate."

"Bingo," KB said, "These are pirates." He took his arm from around her and moved closer to the screen. The pirate looked directly at them before turning away. Maeve stayed back, afraid the image would speak directly to her once again. Oblivious, KB continued, "You thought, what, they'd gone extinct? Hell no. The criminals of the sea have only gotten more sophisticated. I mean, take a look at that equipment and the people working."

With the pirate's back to them, Maeve moved closer to get a better look, curious what her vision was doing on the screen, looking past the divers and the few crew to follow him. "Where are they?"

"Right here, basically in our back yard. It's outside the Bay where the Hudson flows into the Atlantic. Astonishing, right? Fish-farming isn't relegated to a few calm Asian estuaries. This is mammoth, illegal and unethical. But that never stops them," KB said bitterly.

"You think my parents are here? All the way out here?"

KB hesitated. Maeve's parents weren't his number

one priority. He'd have to remember that to get her to cooperate with his plans, he would have to at least pretend interest in hers. "It's not that far and yes, I think they may be drawn here." He neglected to explain that they might have pushed themselves there to get help from the captain, Abigor. KB wasn't sure he could share the fact that their mother Charlotte and, especially Victor, her father, walked the line between Shadow and Light. He doubted she'd believe that they'd dip into Shadow when it suited what Charlotte would call, "the greater good."

Maeve continued searching the screen for signs and questioned, "How will we see them? And what idiot would put pens into the Atlantic? There's a host of huge problems, navigation being the most obvious." She leaned back on her elbows, happy to have spent her entire adulthood in environmental engineering, but noticed KB's bravado had suddenly shifted toward depression. "What are they seeding?" she asked to divert his attention.

"You'll die when I tell you," KB lowered his voice and stretched before he stood and hobbled to the table to search for something among the papers once again. He called over his shoulder, "I've been watching them for a while. I'm pretty sure it's salmon. Seems they're marketing to restaurants in the city. Grounds love eating what's easy, convenient and cheap. And they love seafood." He made quotation marks with his fingers as he continued looking through the papers. "They rarely ask where it comes from. Ground waiters and waitresses either don't know or they lie. So, voila! As we kill the natural habitat for these amazing fish we'll be growing them here, continuing to pollute the water of the Hudson River estuary." He shook his head. "And yes, mom and dad may be there."

Maeve looked closer at the screen, straining to see them, anxious to get down there.

KB was glad to have caught her interest. If she were ever to achieve her potential, she would have to sacrifice her personal goals and relationships to bigger pursuits, like he had. "But that's not the only thing," he said. "Take a good look at the people working. Not so much the divers, although they are being extorted with something to work on this project. But the crew."

Maeve examined the people running around, attaching lines, swabbing decks and said, "Well they are skinny for sure. They don't look much like sailors."

"They're trafficked. These are people from the poorest parts of the world. Mostly from South America on this ship. But it's a formula for pirates the world over. They use them until they can't, letting them die of exhaustion or accidents." KB pulled a second set of plans from the pile and tossed them beside the others as he knelt to lean more closely into the set.

He was searching for a face he'd known from Peru, Marissa, the wife of a Ground he'd worked closely with and befriended. But he'd complicated things by having an affair with her. He'd never regret it, however. He could still smell her hair and if he closed his eyes, could feel the touch of her skin. Their conversations into the night discussing democracy and revolutionaries had given him hope for evolution of the Grounds into light. In fact, he'd hoped to confront his friend Pablo and take her away.

But Marissa denied him. "And what will I do with you when I abandon my family and country? Try to keep up? My magic is our relationship. You'll resent me when all I can conjure is a warm place in your heart. No. We'll end up hating each other. Let's treasure what we have. Pablo will never suspect this isn't his baby and he'll be a better father than you could be."

The last sentence stung to this day. Worse, politics and a coup overtook his personal drama and KB helplessly watched his friend Pablo be convicted of crimes against the state, forbidden to interfere by the Light council. In that moment, he'd vowed to take Marissa and his child away to safety. He'd commit to being a father after all.

But instead he'd been summoned by the Lights and convicted himself. Banned from visiting Peru and the southern provinces ever again, he could only commune with Marissa and her son in moments when the baby's mind was still so open he could easily get in through seance and meditation. He knew it was a boy but gleaned they were struggling and felt the pangs of a promise unfulfilled. He desperately wanted to make everything right. The then newly born baby would be about the right age to be sold into slavery among these workers now. His mother, lacking the perpetual youth enjoyed by Lights, would be an older woman. Marissa had shut him out years ago and, although a Ground, she'd shown distinctly elevated mental strength to block KB. Even his sister Kitty couldn't help and advised him to let it go. Marissa had closed that door and would not reopen it.

But he hoped to get a foot in through the boy. If he could only reestablish contact with him and then later with his mom he knew he could help them. However, as the child grew and his mind closed with social conditioning and perhaps the counsel of his mother, KB had more difficulty establishing connection. Yet he continued searching.

Not finding recognition in any of the vacant eyes that swabbed the deck, he absentmindedly related to Maeve, "And they dump the bodies into those pens when the poor bastards finally let go. What the fish don't eat washes eventually to shore, here," he drew Maeve's attention to the plans he'd laid on the floor and explained, "In this estuary by the Hudson, which, by the way, has been making some great comebacks of late."

"Was that your work? Saving people from pirates?" Maeve asked.

"My work is to save humanity," he said flatly. Annoyed that she still didn't quite understand the magnitude of their responsibility he added, "Yours too, by the way. And to help them understand they are part of the earth, not separate from her or each other."

Maeve was beginning to understand that it wasn't just about saving her parents. Although that was her priority, she felt slightly more patient with him as he continued over the roar of the TV, "Places like this system, these bays and tidal rivers that meet the Atlantic Ocean are where life begins, or ends. Take this project, for example," he said, caressing a spot on the plans, "New York's recovering Jamaica Bay Wildlife Refuge, neighbor to the busiest harbor in the entire world, Upper New York Bay. It's an amazing confluence of the natural and the commercial and this system works overtime to clear the contamination from those activities."

"I know," Maeve agreed. "These estuaries are amazing."

She glanced at the plans quickly before screams drew them both back to the television. KB kneeled as they witnessed a wave crest the railing and take two men overboard. The captain ran to starboard and screamed to the divers who submerged once again, hopefully to help the men.

"It's a shit show out there," he said, "Have a look at this."

Maeve couldn't pull her attention from the scene and asked him impatiently, "So, my parents are out there somewhere?"

"Somewhere close, yes. It's all connected. The river runs to the sea, right? And they are part of that system now. So yes. These guys, especially Captain Abigor, practice pulling energy, a lot like a vampire draws blood. They'll be drawn towards them."

He neglected to tell her that he was certain since he knew the captain well. Abigor was his brother and they'd been fighting for centuries. KB suspected his mother would not only be drawn there but be trying to get to him for help. Victor too. He'd pushed KB away when he married Charlotte but had taken Abigor under his wing, calling him son and learning dark secrets from him that he pulled into his Light politics.

"Abigor," Maeve mumbled. "What kind of name is that?"

"Christian terror, the demon of war. His real name is Luke but he's known far and wide by Abigor," KB explained as Maeve looked for recognizable faces among the waves or among the crew.

"If our mother and your father don't get pulled out to sea or taken in by these pirates, the currents will eventually bring them to the calm estuary. It's beautiful and a resting place for the lost."

He traced his fingers dreamily over one area on the drawings outstretched on the floor as he reminisced, "We had hundreds of people from the large cities all around this estuary like New York City and Newark seeding oysters over here. It was great to watch people living in cities that have been polluting for ages step up and actually do something to ameliorate the effects. By developing community and educating, we've changed practices. Next month we'll be seeding the salt marsh and over the summer kids will come here to learn and enjoy the space. Together we can improve the estuary's health. Cool stuff really. Grounds, heck, including the Port Authority, have been receptive. No one wants to live by a dead ocean."

Maeve nodded absentmindedly, searching for her parents among the slaves wandering the screen, frustrated by her inability to see more.

KB recognized more than one of the slaves from his

battles in Peru but none shared Marissa's high cheekbones or full lips. Nor his signature dark wavy hair.

Maeve pulled his attention away from the desperate faces urging, "Let's go then. I can't take it that they could be so close and I'm here watching," she searched for the words before spitting, "An antique TV."

The storm and yelling on the screen continued as KB took her hand and explained. "Hey, it's an amazing set. Age has nothing to do with it." He smiled. "But now," he paused to move his injured foot that was healing quickly, "Take just a second to realize how through small actions, like reducing consumption and waste from the ships, modifying routes to avoid migrating species and even planting beds of oysters to filter pollutants from the water and stabilize the shore, we've made this place a safe haven. They'll be waiting here. If the pirates don't get them first, that is."

Maeve listened to his rantings. He was a person no one had acknowledged for eons. He'd worked these areas incessantly, without accolades or, it seemed, much help apart from his northern sisters and the few group efforts he'd planned and organized.

She noticed the stains on his teeth and fingers from coffee and tobacco and long hours perusing experimental data. She sympathized and knew he deserved to be heard. But she needed to act and demanded, "So first to the ship? We need to get there."

He nodded, stood and tossed some food into the aquarium that had settled peacefully before he encouraged her, "Yeah. We'll get there before someone else harvests them, either at sea or here in the estuary."

As the TV called his attention once again, he explained, "There are still loads of small subsistence fishermen in the area and, of course, these pirates. You know, if they're successful, this project will overload the system with pollution from suffering slaves and the farmed fish. The stuff they feed them, full of antibiotics and chemicals, falls to the ocean floor from their poo. There's lots of that too since they're all packed in these pens, humans and fish, living in horrible conditions. I'd rather not have to pull mom and dad from that muck. It's damaging." He was still unsure how to tell his little sister that her parents walked the line between Shadow and Light or that Abigor, the evil pirate she was watching, was her half-brother.

So he didn't. Instead, he shifted his weight to his now healed leg, touched his head to feel that the lump had subsided and, wanting her to help him rescue the entire scenario not merely her parents, said, "Yeah, let's go."

Chapter 6

"Remember, dim your light," KB cautioned, picking up speed as they crossed unseen like a blur over the state line on a route KB obviously knew well. "We'll cross into Manhattan at the George Washington Bridge. We want that side at the end but I'd like to consult a friend of mine who runs a great diner," he called back to her as they approached the city.

"Makes sense," she agreed, not imagining he'd try to divert their plan. Her stomach growled at the thought of food and she was happy they'd stop. While training in martial arts with Mary, the wise tough old woman had explained on more than one occasion, "It's difficult to manifest on an empty stomach." And Maeve wanted desperately to manifest a way to save her parents. "You have money?" she asked KB.

"I'll figure that out when the bill comes," he said.

"Who have I become," she wondered as she thought of adding "running out on bills" to her repertoire of "super powers."

They slowed their pace and walked around a corner where a neon sign in script read, "The Last Cup." Maeve swore she saw their names scroll across the cup with the word "welcome" as they entered but the text disappeared as KB pushed the door open. And she swore she heard the echo of their names announced as they entered the neighborhood diner. "Did you hear that?" she asked KB. But he ignored her as he looked for a booth.

Her stomach growled in front of the classic glass door fridge full of pies at the entrance. But these pies were moving and softly squeaking "eat me" when she'd look their way. Slightly repulsed, she moved her gaze to the counter and saw the sign for "bottomless coffee" had a cup with literally no bottom. Hot coffee came directly from the drip machine suspended above the sign through the cup and into a thermos pot on the counter below. When the waitress took the pot, the drip stopped until she came back. Once she put it down the cycle started again. Fascinated, Maeve glanced at the chalkboard menu behind the counter that listed the specials and asked KB, "What is this place?"

"Don't tell me you've never been to a diner," he joked as he found a booth by the window. "Gotta love Jersey," he continued as if it were all so normal.

"Nothing ever like this. The pies called to me," Maeve told him.

"Yeah. They look good right?"

"I'm not explaining," Maeve told him, "They have mouths and they spoke, not just calling with their looks. And our names were announced when we walked in the door."

"AI," he told her and winked as the waitress arrived before he could elaborate.

Maeve quizzed her about the food and the pies and finally ordered exactly what KB had: omelet with free range eggs. She prayed it wouldn't talk back to her on the plate. She was hungry. As the waitress walked away, she asked KB, "This place is humming with otherworldliness. Is that what you'd like to show me?"

"Yes and no. Yes, I'd like to show you the magical beauty in the everyday. That's what the Grounds don't get. Over time, they've mixed it all up. You know this is an old neighborhood and they all go through cycles, right? Some, less drastic than others. But right now, there's a push from the Shadows to kill these areas. More malls, more closed spaces, gated communities, less small town feel. And these small communities are a huge part of the cohesive force we have as humans. That's the force that's keeping your parents from disintegrating. We hold on and the memories we keep alive help that happen.

Shoot, Walmart isn't going to know the old woman who lives upstairs and may need help if you don't see her walking her dog. But this waitress will," he told her as the waitress put plates on the table and asked, "More coffee?" as she filled their cups regardless. Maeve lifted her cup to see the bottom, still wondering about the display and saw that the cup was indeed bottomless. She touched it to see if it were glass but her finger dipped into the hot liquid. "Ouch," she cried, surprised. The coffee didn't spill through but rather was suspended there magically.

"Did you see this?" she asked KB.

"Cool right?

"But how do they do that?"

"No idea," he smiled.

Maeve picked up her fork, still wondering about the coffee and pies, ready to dig in but KB took her hand and said, "Let's say grace first."

Surprised, she mumbled, "Right. I can't believe I forgot," even though she never in her entire life said grace. She put her fork on the table and took a moment of gratitude with KB before they ate.

"It'll save you," KB said as he cut his omelet.

"What," Maeve said, carefully lifting the coffee cup to her lips wondering how nothing was dripping out.

"Gratitude," he told her, "For all of it," as she shoveled a bite into her mouth greedily.

She admitted, "I was hungrier than I thought. But KB, how will you change that? How will you help people to understand and protect these small community spaces, neighborhood places and parks?"

The bill floated from the waitress's pad to the table on an unseen breeze. Maeve caught it and once again questioned, "Did you see that?" KB ignored her and she surreptitiously checked the exits, looking for a quick way out when they couldn't pay.

"And the huge spaces, like Palisades," he told her. "Community will preserve nature and us. It's all about education. You'll see." He wiped his mouth with the cloth napkin. "If people only believe how great material things are, they never get to know anything else. Anyway, the guy who owns this diner is a magician when it comes to community outreach and organization."

"Explains the magic around us anyway," Maeve interjected.

"We'll talk to him about your parents and the project. After, we'll cross into Manhattan, down Riverside Drive and get a boat out to the harbor from Battery Park. I know a captain we can stay with there."

"Wait a minute," Maeve interrupted, "He'll know about my parents?"

"He's connected. You know, it's big news what happened to them. They're important to the Light hierarchy. I can't believe you never realized that," he told her flatly.

She wondered herself but had honestly never thought of much outside what they could do for her. Now was her chance to show her parents what she could do in return.

KB continued, "We know they're around the harbor. The water runs there. We'll find them while we research the horror that's happening offshore. With the advice we'll get here and some help, we'll change it all and start something that not only saves mom and dad but pushes the shadows out of power. It will all come together." He allowed himself a snicker. "Win-win, I think you say in the corporate world."

She finished her eggs and put down her fork a little too hard. "So where's your friend with the advice?" she asked, impatient to get going. "You think my parents are in danger of being pulled into it? This project with the pens?"

Suddenly a racket started with bells tinkling and voices echoing saoiste or "boss" over and over. Then a husky male voice cut it off and called, "KB Good to see you, man."

KB turned to greet the tall man who literally floated toward them. "Samuel! Even better to see you." His feet gracefully returned to earth as KB stood to wrap his arms around his massive shoulders and receive a bear hug in return. When the burly magician released him, he introduced Maeve, saying, "This is a relative of mine from way back, Maeve. She's helping me with a few things."

Samuel extended his hand, "A pleasure." His coffee colored hand overwhelmed Maeve's; hers so small, his like the bear claw she'd witnessed up north where she'd trained. As he relaxed the hand shake, he saw the bill on the table, waved his opposite hand over it and sent it floating back to the waitress who tucked it into her pad. "You know you don't pay here," he scolded KB, who smiled and bowed his head.

"Hey, hear about that latest initiative to tear all this down?" Samuel said as he slid into their booth and drew an arc with his arm to indicate the restaurant and the neighborhood. As he did so, Maeve swore she saw the arc he drew outlined in a light that emanated from his elegant fingertips. She quietly listened, fascinated by this magical man.

"I thought that died a while ago," KB replied.

"Resurrected." Samuel said. He shook his head. "It never stops. I find it exhausting and annoying." He turned to Maeve and asked, "So young lady, what brings you to this side of the tracks?"

Before she could answer, they heard the grinding of a car hitting another in the street in front of them. Every face in the diner turned as the two cars stopped in the street and the passenger of the car behind got out to talk to the driver who'd been rear ended. Maeve's eyes opened wider and her jaw dropped slightly when she recognized him. It was Kevin, the gangster who'd tried to kill her and who she'd left for dead after the battle in upstate. He immediately started shouting at the woman they'd hit. A bandage still covered half his face from where KB, in the form of a snake, had bitten him. You could see it was still oozing, the gauze bandage moist in the center. A police car pulled around the corner and Maeve mouthed to KB, "It's them."

Mark stayed seated in the car making a call as one police officer separated Kevin from the woman driver who'd started to cry. "That wound will never heal," KB commented bemused, as the second officer knocked on the window to Mark. "And those two just won't go away," he commented.

"You know those two thugs?" Samuel asked. "They've been around here lately looking for something. What they need is a good doctor. Especially the one with crutches," he nodded toward the scene as Mark got out of the car with difficulty and spoke to the police.

Maeve asked, "Should we confront them?" Her hands were shaking and she realized it was anticipation, not fear.

KB assessed the situation; the police, the crowd of onlookers, the now nearly hysterical woman and Kevin's volatile energy as the officer held him back, ready to arrest him. "It's not the right time. Now we know they're around. It's a good moment to get ahead of them. If they're looking for us, they'll visit you Samuel. Put them off, will you?" he asked as he stuffed another bite into his mouth. Samuel nodded as he continued, "By the way, what do you hear of that project down river in the bay? The one for fish farming out there."

"There was a hearing a while ago. They presented that idea for farming on the Bay. Comical, really. Too many risks and variables. But you know, they painted the picture they wanted and thought we'd eat it. It was voted down. Nearly unanimously."

"Who voted for it?" KB pulled his coat back on, getting ready to hit the road once again.

"There's a small group of Eastern Europeans, relatively new to the city. They were there to support it. I'm nearly certain they were investors," Samuel answered. He shook his head in disbelief.

"What's the pro? It's got to have huge capital investment," KB continued to wonder. Maeve was peripherally watching the scene in the street as Mark was now standing with his cane, arguing with the police as he tried to calm his partner down. She swore the voices of the pies had gotten louder as they too had started fighting among themselves, "Eat me. Eat me. I'm so delicious." The drama made it difficult to follow the conversation.

Samuel noticed and waved his hand in their direction. They became regular pie slices once again. Smiling at Maeve he said, "They can get overly enthusiastic," then he turned to the scene outside and told her, "That's not worth your energy. Don't worry about them for now. Back to this proposal in the harbor. You know, the savings on transport is a huge plus, I mean they'll basically pull fish from the water directly to the table in restaurants."

"Gives 'buy local' a whole new meaning." Maeve

followed KB's lead and slid out of the booth toward the door.

"There's no rent. Its use of public space for private gain. So, the profit margin would've been huge. They weren't at all happy about the denial and they've appealed. But I haven't heard from Ted, that guy with the Save the Harbor group, remember him?" KB nodded and Samuel continued, "Anyway, he said we'd won but disappeared after. I need to check on him, come to think of it. He hasn't been by," Samuel mused.

"I've got a hunch they started," KB told him. "Maeve, let's go out the back." He smiled as he cast a glance to the street to see the police putting Kevin into the back of the squad car and handing Mark a ticket as the tow truck pulled up.

Samuel escorted them through the kitchen asking, "What makes you say that? Don't tell me you've been spying again. And any word from your mother? I haven't heard from her in awhile."

KB knew Samuel and his mother were more than good friends and he didn't disapprove. He didn't approve either. He'd come to terms with Charlotte's infidelities as a part of who she was. But he wasn't sure how Maeve would take it so decided to let Maeve discover her mom's loose interpretation of marriage on her own. He winked and told Samuel, "Yeah, I take a peak now and then. And mom is why we're heading down to check it out. You must have heard we had a conflict awhile ago? How she saved us but was caught in the crossfire. She's dissolved into the flow with her husband Victor, Maeve's dad."

Samuel looked at Maeve, "You're Victor and Charlotte's girl. I should have paid more attention but yes, you have her eyes. And yes, I heard about it. It was big gossip in our Saturday adoption clinic for months. I wondered if they'd contacted you is all. Don't worry, you'll intercept them there in the sea. But be careful. These aren't your average immigrants. KB, you know that. They're powerful Shadows. The eastern bloc mafia's been in town for a while now and this is a new wave. They don't take interference in their business lightly and they've joined with some old wave that you're familiar with."

He waited for KB's reaction but they continued to walk as if he'd known everything. Samuel wondered if they in fact understood the magnitude of the situation as they passed through the kitchen and the waitress handed him a bag with takeaway. "I packed this for you. Manifesting energies can get stuck in the city. So much going on," Samuel said and winked at Maeve as he took both her hands in his. "It will work out," he assured her knowingly and she felt confident and taken care of as he did. "But for now, put that food into your special backpack. My number's on the bag. And you," he punched a finger into KB's chest. "Remember, you've been on the receiving end of that struggle before."

Maeve pushed the bag into her pack and wiggled past KB to open the door. "We need to do something. My parents can't stay dissolved and KB showed me, people will keep going until you stand up to them, even if that means killing them, like with those two thugs out front. I guess I should have been more careful to finish them off when I had the chance."

Samuel's brow tightened as he understood this young woman who he knew had been so protected and naive was now fine with killing to get what she believed was right. It saddened him that she'd grown so strong. He preferred the little girl Charlotte was always bragging about after their love making. He'd seen pictures of her wide innocent eyes. Now he saw them filled with righteousness and told her, "I understand your perspective and what's happened to you. But there are always two sides to the story. And each being is valuable. You may need to fight to survive, but there are always alternatives to killing. Never forget that. Those two may serve some greater purpose in the long run."

He directed his next comment to KB and told him, "Believe it or not, they're selling the idea that the ocean can neutralize all the organic material that's a by-product of this industry. It's a joke. But people want to believe it. Just like you wanted to believe those men would go away and leave you alone," he said to Maeve.

"How'd you know?" Maeve asked incredulously.

"I know lots of things," he said to her, smiling . "Like that these particular developers will continue to lie and give guarantees they cannot uphold until they get what they want."

KB added quietly, "They can't guarantee anything, least of all the sea's ability to handle their input. Even though they're farther out in the ocean they'll still affect the harbor."

KB followed Maeve outside and into the alleyway as he pulled the hood of his sweatshirt over his head saying, "So, Samuel, you are so right. The potential for added-value usage of fish wastes like fertilizer or bio-gas is underexploited. But this project has got to go. We'll make that happen."

Maeve's eyes widened and she felt the thrill of anticipation in her gut. She suddenly regretted not stopping in the bathroom before they'd left.

"OK," Samuel drew the word out slowly. "If you're going to mix it up, talk to Sarah. You remember her, right?"

"Smart, independent and beautiful? Yeah, vaguely," KB joked. "We're on our way there."

Samuel smiled and shook his head. Maeve felt a tinge of jealousy but buried it, reminding herself that KB was her brother from generations ago. Still the comment stung somehow.

"I was hoping you'd give me her number?" KB asked.

"Work purposes only," Samuel joked as he took out his phone and said, "You still using only burners?"

KB nodded yes and added, "You're crazy if you don't."

Maeve whined to Samuel, "I don't even have a phone anymore. I'm not allowed."

Samuel laughed, gauging the emotional landscape between the two before saying, "I'll write it down for you then." He wrote the number on the back of the bill. Then he reminded Maeve in fatherly fashion, "I know he won't let you have a phone. But find one and call me if you need anything, ok? If you can't get to a phone, I'm intuitive," he said seriously, "Focus on me and I'll know."

Before he turned to go back, he added, "If your

parents want to be found, they'll be in the ocean, not the estuary. But don't be surprised if they're not ready to see you. Or allowed, for that matter. There's a council over theirs."

Maeve studied her palms, not wanting to cry, afraid her emotions would betray her.

"I know that's not what you wanted to hear but you'll see them again," he assured her and took KB's hand saying, "It's great to see you man. They won't be in the estuary. Go directly to the ship. You may find your Peruvians there too."

The two friends hugged. "Thanks for the meal, the discussion and the help, as always."

"How do you know about my parents?" she asked before she turned to go.

Samuel gave her a hug, smiled and said, "I do more than run this diner, Maeve. I was part of the decision to hold them as water and save you. Your father was overreacting. But his anger would have destroyed you and KB, two Lights we need desperately in this moment and for several futures. Remember, there are many agendas at play here. Your's is only one of them. Be careful, even with the sisters." Maeve's eyes widened and she realized this was where they'd run when they did errands.

"We spoke about you," Samuel confided. "In fact, Kitty sat right there putting the finishing touches on that most amazing backpack. And who do you think makes those amazing pies?"

"The sister's pies never talked back," Maeve joked with him.

Samuel laughed and continued, "Regardless, we all agree. We need to control things before they trigger events we may not be able to stop, especially in terms of cleaning our own house." He put a hand on her shoulder. "You did the right thing letting them fall. KB was and is your best choice for help. But be careful with everyone," he cautioned, "Trust your intuition and your guides."

With even KB? Maeve wondered as she watched the friends hug once again before they walked down the alley to avoid the street full of people who had no clue of what was going on a few miles out in their harbor.

Samuel called after them, "Live for the big fight. We can only fix this if we're smarter, regardless who's stronger."

They started running and Maeve commented, "Samuel is pretty cool."

KB smiled. "You have no idea. He's an amazing asset and friend. But he has his agenda too. Just like us all. Stay connected to your inner voice. That's our final guide. So tell me when yours speaks up," he called as they ran toward the city.

Samuel watched them leave, wondering how he would reconcile his goal of rescuing Charlotte but keeping Victor trapped as liquid. He alone realized that Charlotte might believe life with her Shadow son might be perfect as it served the goal of letting Grounds find their own way. After all, that was Charlotte's constant mantra, "They'll find their way if we let them fall." She didn't concern herself that it would be through hunger, slavery and destruction. Or that they might never manage to pull themselves out of it.

Besides, he was ready for the formal connection of marriage so they could take over the council. With Charlotte at his side they'd be most powerful. After all, he'd been her lover for over a century and he brought his own level of power to the table. She'd never leave him. He considered himself her match and he was finally ready. Victor was the only barrier so he simply had to go, regardless if he were Maeve's father.

"Godspeed," he called after his friends as his feet once again left the ground and he floated back to his diner to order pie.

Chapter 7

Everything was happening too fast and not fast enough. The too fast stuff wasn't advancing her personal goals and the not fast enough was making her crazy. Sure, meeting Samuel made her acutely aware of how much she didn't know, especially about Lights. Maeve knew she had lots to learn but time was slipping through her fingers. And now, another player and probably another lesson from this woman named Sarah. One step forward, two steps back. She wished she'd left alone to find Kitty when she had the chance. She was getting more and more into KB's plan to save the ocean and the slaves and farther it seemed from any plan to save her parents. Or was she? She reminded herself they were connected. They had to be. Or what was she doing with these people.

She sped past KB wanting to escape the entire scenario. But he caught her easily. Annoyed, she teased in a sing-song voice, "Call Sarah, will you?" and then let her voice return to its normal pitch to add, "Maybe then you'll give me a break."

"Ah, right," he sighed, pretending to have forgotten the call. They slowed to a stop just before the George Washington bridge. Maeve waited as he took a phone from one pocket, reached into the other for a battery and assembled them quickly as traffic moved noisily past them.

"Special pockets?" Maeve said with a smirk.

KB nodded with a smile.

"Then why am I carrying

everything?" Maeve asked.

KB shrugged, "No idea," as he dialed Sarah's number, grinning.

Sarah answered right away. "Samuel said you'd call. Meet me at Battery park. The dock where the ferries leave for Miss Liberty. Remember my boat? The Zephyr?" she asked.

"'Course," he answered before she hung up. He told Maeve, "Let's go," as he separated the phone and the battery once again and they ran toward Manhattan.

A blur of people, cars, sights and sound passed as they nearly flew down Amsterdam Ave past hip shops and restaurants, weaving on and off the sidewalk to dodge people and cars. They moved like a flash onto Broadway where the streets cleared a bit but were still jammed with people who only noticed a breeze or a nudge passing them. The pair moved past City Hall and past where the twin towers had been to find Battery Park.

The sky opened as they left the skyscrapers behind and entered the park on New York Harbor. They both slowed and inhaled the fresher sea air as ships, boats, the odd helicopter and the Statue of Liberty vied for attention a few meters off the coast. Two skateboarders passed disrespectfully close and Maeve smiled as she inhaled the blend of marijuana and sweat. Still fascinated by the city, she nostalgically took it all in; the few benches filled with groups of day trippers taking selfies; the office workers hustling to get out or back in time; the homeless people poking into trash or asking for a hand out and the dog walkers scooping poo after their pups. "Feels like home," she told him.

KB smiled, shook his head and said, "So unaware. That was you a few months back, right?"

"Not quite but, yeah," she agreed, remembering her past life. "But we can build that awareness. It's the first step toward change and our job as 'aware' humans, you know?" Maeve reminded him, making quotation marks with her hands.

They scanned the dock for the Zephyr and simultaneously noticed a woman in a flannel shirt and cover-alls sitting at the helm of a refurbished lobster boat, reading. Feeling their presence, she looked up and smiled showing a gap between her front teeth that made her even more lovely. KB's energy shifted and became lighter and more attractive. Maeve marveled at a man's ability to be so transparent. Even his voice became smoother by the time they reached the boat.

He asked, "How's it going Sarah? Remember me?"

And she also marveled at how it bothered her ever so slightly to have him flirt with this other woman. "He's your brother," she scolded herself and although she didn't want a romantic relationship with him, she realized she didn't want to share. She needed him to get to her parents and didn't want him distracted by this female captain of the high seas. It was difficult enough to focus him on the project at hand.

Sarah's melodic laugh called her back to the moment as she said matter-of-factly, "Of course I remember you. Don't be ridiculous. It hasn't been that long, KB. Less than a decade." She winked and held out her hand saying genuinely, "Come on board the Zephyr." She had a hoarse voice that gave her a seafarer's credibility and Maeve liked her immediately, even though she didn't want to.

"This is Maeve," KB announced as he stepped over the railing.

"Pleasure, Maeve," Sarah said and extended a hand to help her board as she subtly assessed the slight young woman she saw before her. "Have a seat." She opened a side bench off the transom and leaned on the combing saying. "Talk to me. Then we'll take a ride. But first, kick those street shoes off, will you? I'll get you some proper boots." She went below, tossed up some rubber pull-on boots and called, "Before we head out, you'll need to suit up. It's choppy out there today."

Sarah's direct manner and robust countenance put Maeve at ease and she happily kicked her sneakers off to feel the sun warmed floor that, like the rest of the Zephyr, was clean and trim, everything in its place.

"If it's not," Sarah commented, "you either lose it or it hits you in the head in the worst moment possible."

"You read my mind?" Maeve asked

"You left it wide open girlfriend. You need to work on that out here. Fishermen are gossips and they'll get in where they can," she commented with a smile and pushed a strand of brown hair behind her multi-pierced ear.

"And," KB said, "Behind those beguiling cacao colored eyes, Sarah's a master mind reader. You'll have a hard time blocking her. But I'll show you how." His tone was challenging in a flirty way and Maeve realized that he liked

Sarah. A lot. She also sensed an unavailability about Sarah that made her more interesting.

"We'll see about that. Samuel explained why you're here and gave me some background." She sounded concerned as she asked KB, "You sure you're ready for this? It's more than we've seen for some time."

He didn't reply but he suddenly lost the frivolity he'd cultivated seconds before. "Let me show you something," she said to counter the dark demeanor that had washed over him.

She brought out some charts but reconsidered as the boat swayed back and forth from waves as a ferry passed. "Inside's better," she said, motioning them to follow and taking the map into the berth as she folded open a table. She rolled it out, pulled a few charts from the shelves next to it and said, "Here are several locations where they're placing crates," she pointed to a couple of locations outlined with a red marker. "It's so crazy to be honest. I'd never believe it if I hadn't seen it with my own eyes." The area covered nearly a quarter of the chart. "I don't know how they plan on harvesting but there are so many variables with this that there's got to be more involved. I mean, the financial and environmental losses could be staggering. So, the profit potential must be huge to merit the risk."

"With no investment in land costs or machinery besides boats, crates, personnel like divers and laborers who appear to be slaves, and there's the fish, but that's robbed from the wild, so there's a huge profit motive," KB said.

"But there are loads of less risky places," Sarah explained. "I think there's more. Only each time I get close enough, I get totally blocked. They've put some strong barriers around themselves. Plus, there is them; dark and powerful. Alone, I'm no match for going in."

"It's why we're here," Maeve said, naively confident, "We'll get closer."

"Right. I'll show you how that goes." Sarah stowed the charts and prepared to cast off. "You've been on a boat before?"

Maeve nodded and Sarah said satisfactorily, "Great. Let's go" as she started the engine. KB undid the lines and pushed the bow off the dock as Maeve pulled in the bumpers. Sarah directed Maeve to sit beside her at the helm and KB stood between them, holding the backs of the seats as they headed into New York Harbor.

Chapter 8

"This is the busiest port on the east coast," Sarah explained as she navigated her ship out of New York Harbor. "Between container shipping, tourists and recreational boaters, you need to pay attention. Especially over there," Sarah nodded toward Liberty Island. "I love that place. Everything about it, especially Miss Liberty. But it gets crowded."

Maeve let her go on, although in her life as an environmental engineer she knew all about the port of New York. In fact, after the planes hit the Twin Towers on September 11, 2001, container ships and tankers clogged the port and one of her first engineering jobs was issuing permits for the ships to unload and depart. But that was then, another life. In this life, she was the untested newbie and had to swallow her pride.

Sarah looked at her quizzically. "Sorry," she said, "I didn't know."

"You've got to stop that," Maeve said, laughing, but secretly glad that Sarah could read her mind now and know that she had lots of knowledge to bring to this expedition too.

"I always hate when men minimize me, but it's worse when we women do it to each other. I apologize," Sarah said.

"Accepted," Maeve said.

The boat sliced through the choppy water as they watched tourists coming and going on the green lawn that led to the immense concrete base of the Statue of Liberty. Maeve thought how comic the mimic crowns of stars and fake torches donned by tourists seemed as they posed for photos in front of the landmark monument to immigration. She saw her former self in most of them and sighed, "They have no idea," as Sarah called over the engine, "We're heading out of the upper bay now. East is the Jamaica Bay restoration area. Over there," she pointed towards a coastal area with marsh grass and calmer seas. "Your favorite, KB. An amazing example of urban ecosystem renewal. Another day we'll take a drive around Staten Island and have a look at the saltmarsh restorations there." She paused and adjusted their course before she turned to ask, "How long are you around?"

"I get a little crazy in the city after a couple of days," KB said.

Sarah looked at Maeve, "You've got nowhere to go. Why not hang out with me and get to know the area better? Today's reconnaissance. But this project needs a plan." She steered them around the barrier beach of Jamaica Bay and into the Atlantic saying, "Hold on. The water gets rougher out here."

"In case you hadn't intuited," Maeve emphasized the word, referring to Sarah's mind-reading skills, "I'm here to find my parents. This project takes a back seat for me unless it's obviously connected."

Sarah didn't answer and Maeve searched the deeper water for signs of her parents. "I mean," she continued, "They could be right below us." The sea outside the harbor

71

had a different texture. The color had shifted from light blue green to deep dark blue and Maeve felt the shift in depth. It made her feel less grounded and nervous.

"That's a past life experience," Sarah commented matter-of-factly shifting the conversation. "You drowned once and not easily. You hung on in the ocean for a while with an amazing will to survive."

KB explained to Maeve's surprise, "It's her thing. Besides being a mind-reader, she's a seer. She can tell you all about what happened in your past. Things you may not remember."

"I'd like to be clairvoyant, but the past is my gift," Sarah called, her voice muffled once again by the engine. "It helps lots of Lights overcome uncanny fears. Knowing they were burned at the stake, for example, explains some present day fears. Take KB, there are things in this life he can't deal with that come from past lives of persecution and torture."

KB cut her off. "Let's stay focused on the present, please."

The propeller groaned as the rolling sea lifted it out of the water and a wave crashed over the bow. Feeling seasick, Maeve went outside. But before she could sit down, she got goosebumps and smelled a scent she remembered from her training with the sisters. She scanned the horizon, feeling Shadow presence and then called out, "Over there, the way the whole area changes, like there's a thick window in front of us. That's them, right?"

"Not bad for a novice. How do you feel?" Sarah asked.

"Besides nauseous? It's pushing me away, like I'm up

against firm jello but also repelled, emotionally as much as physically. I feel a deep desire to turn away. Is that how it works with boats too? It literally pushes them around with what, magnets?"

"I'm still not sure but you're right. It's a sort of magnetic protection they use with their cloaking skills. These guys are sophisticated. It keeps traffic from even entering the area. I need to research more but I know it confuses navigational instruments. Look, they say we're still on a clear course," Sarah said, touching her radar, "but we're not. I know that. "Even more interesting, it'll keep the instruments back on course once we pass. You'd never know we'd been off course or so close to this ship we can almost see it. It's incredible. But it'll eventually cause accidents. Imagine, these huge tankers, on auto pilot and off course without any idea or warning. When they collide," she shook her head and took a deep breath as she continued, "Well, I don't want to even think about it."

KB commented, "Two oil tankers colliding, that'll top the charts."

"Nightmare describes it best, with widespread impact." Sarah intuitively managed the boat's course saying, "There's a small hole over to the west where we can get a peek inside. I'm without instruments now so if you see anything coming let me know."

She skillfully turned the boat to drive along the blurry wall of the ships' cover. It was like riding along a fogged window. The waves slapped the side of the boat that rolled with them as the three passengers stood with legs wide, knees bent, mimicking their undulations and holding on as they passed a blurry Talisman painted on the transom of the ship.

"Not sure this talisman is bringing anyone luck," KB said, gripping the railing as he continued, "You should come to my cave and watch with us on the TV sometime, not so risky."

Sarah smiled and asked, "Are you flirting with me?" enjoying the idea before she pulled firmly on the wheel to keep them from crashing into the blur. Again, Maeve felt a twinge of jealousy as Sarah called gleefully, "Hands on is so much more fun."

"You obviously don't have my past lives," he countered.

Sea conditions weren't optimal for Maeve's seasickness. Sarah noticed her nearly green face and said, "Woah, girlfriend, breathe deeply. Watch the horizon. We'll head back into the waves shortly. Go out back for some air but be careful."

Maeve helped herself to the back of the boat, gripping the railing. She sat on the deck, leaned her head back and closed her eyes. The spray from the ocean and the sea air helped her focus on not throwing up. But it wasn't enough. She started to convulse and stood to vomit over the edge as an ice-colored blue green wave crashed their side. It came over the railing, filling the boat and splashing onto the other side. As it receded, the swell scooped her off her feet and cradled her quickly into the frigid sea.

The icy, dark Atlantic Ocean smashed against her

body. Everything tingled and started to numb from the cold. She panicked and inhaled sea water. Flailing her arms and legs, trying to cough and tasting a mix of salt and vomit, Maeve struggled to the surface to breathe as another mischievous wave pushed her head under, barely allowing her any air. A numb peace was overtaking her body with the cold yet she opened her eyes under the water, not wanting to surrender.

Suddenly she noticed something, or someone. It was a light, shining brightly, deep down in front of her. It looked vaguely like two octopi. One was in a container and the other floating above it, dark tentacles undulating in the sea. As she strained to stay underwater and see more clearly, the image above turned toward her to show, not an octopus, but the same face that had summoned her at West Point, the same pirate she'd watched with KB from his cave: Abigor. That same rugged, scarred apparition laughed at her once again.

"*Cuimhnigh ar do chumhachtaí*," he reminded her gleefully in Irish but continued in English nearly reprimanding her after telling her to remember her power. "It's not your time, you see. We have work to do together. Join me. Those two buffoons you're with have no idea. I have your parents. I can help you." Then he called again in Irish, "*Bí liom*," She understood he was calling her to join him as his voice trailed off and the vision dissipated into bubbles, leaving only an echo that chastised, "Charlotte and Victor wonder what you're doing? Taking so much time."

The last statement was like a slap to the face. Maeve

searched the water for him, her eyes bulging from the sting of salty sea. But she only saw the graying octopus in the crate below. Desperate to breathe, she shook her head and kicked her feet to surface. As she did, she found a rhythm and her strength. Finally, like a dolphin, she catapulted from the cold water, inhaling deeply and riding the immense waves rather than being overwhelmed by them. Feeling part of the ocean, rather than separate from it, she smiled and screamed, *"Níl mo théarma caite,"* in Irish as she realized it was not her time to go. Not yet anyway.

The air felt relatively warm on her body for a second before she dove back in, this time deep, intuitively clearing her ears as she let the depth pull her toward the light. Below the surface, the water was calm, undulating softly in the depth. She moved closer to the light again, searching for the face. But she only discovered a machine vibrating softly past the place where the octopus lay. She swallowed to keep from inhaling and willed herself to withstand another few seconds to observe and get closer.

The machine had porthole windows on both ends and along the sides. Two hoses connected it to the surface, probably to the boats above. Holding her depth, moving up and down with the waves, she squinted to see inside and noticed two robotic hands taking what appeared to be samples. When the hands extended toward her, she hid behind some seaweed for a second longer before kicking to the surface. Breaching at the horizon, she inhaled deeply and rode a wave toward the Zephyr, moving in and out of the water like a playful dolphin. She overtook the boat and nudged herself to the bow with a kick before she pulled herself onto the wet slippery deck.

Sarah screamed "Hold on," as she steered the boat along the waves and then commanded, "KB, pull her in here."

Already at the bow, KB grabbed Maeve's arm at the bicep and pulled her along the deck and over to the side where he took her waist and hoisted her into the undulating boat asking, "What happened?"

Maeve spit water from her mouth and laughed, "That was incredible. Did you see it?"

"No," Sarah called sternly from the helm, "But you both need to see this." She pulled the boat to starboard and around the shadows' cloaking to a hole in the invisible net they had cast around them. She yelled over the din of the stormy sea, "It's their umbilical cord. This hole connects them to their source. We can't go too close, or we could get sucked in. But we can see," and she let the word hang.

A huge, oversized version of the lobster boat they were in sat low in the water, covered with fish pens. Divers were attaching lines, checking them and attaching nets to secure locks and floatation systems. There was a frenetic, bustling energy around the deck.

KB groaned when he saw the Styrofoam crates and shook his head. "Just what we need more of in the world, Styrofoam."

"That's the least of it," Sarah said.

The bow space was covered so the crew had space to work, sleep and eat. There were 6 men at the helm in the middle of the ship discussing charts.

"Dim your light," KB said. "One turn of their heads and we'll be found. You're both glowing. And up your cloaking," he commanded.

"A couple minutes more and we'll get out of here," Sarah assured him, holding the boat steady against the waves.

Maeve noticed something in the distance high above them. It was a speck moving in different directions against the clouds that were filling the sky. "Shit," she said, "It's a drone. There, above and outside their bubble."

Sarah and KB saw it too.

KB commanded, "We've got to go."

"Not so fast. Take the helm," Sarah ordered as she reached into the cockpit and pulled out a rifle commenting,

"Seriously?" Maeve asked.

"A girl's got to take care of herself on the open seas. Pirates everywhere." She raised the piece to her shoulder, rode the undulating waves to aim and pulled the trigger. The small piece fell from the sky.

Before she could bring the rifle down, Maeve dove off the boat and literally ran on the water to retrieve it. She came back to the boat with the device seconds later.

"Well done," Sarah told Maeve as she took it from her soaking wet hands and said, "There are towels downstairs. Dry off before you freeze to death."

"Time's up. Especially now that you've shot their spy out of the sky. Let's get out of here," KB commanded.

Sarah nodded, turned the wheel and said, "Yeah. But

at least you have an idea what's going on and what we're up against."

"That we do," KB said as Maeve came upstairs with a towel around her neck.

Sarah hit full throttle and said, "Let me show you something more inspiring on the way back." She turned the boat slightly north of New York Harbor toward the Jamaica Bay Wildlife Preserve as behind them an oversized image of Abigor's face rose over where his ship was still invisible. His hair undulating in the breeze and his gold hoop earrings moving back and forth as he watched them head home.

Chapter 9

Sarah slowed and turned the engine off letting the Zephyr float on the incoming waves while she daydreamed about walking the shore with her husband, collecting shells of horseshoe crabs and then discovering a diamond terrapin turtle. They'd been discussing how the horseshoe crab wasn't a crab at all but an arthropod more related to spiders than crabs. As they both bent over the turtle, he'd called her a nerd, then dropped to both knees to kneel in the shallow water and propose marriage. People always asked her why she wouldn't take up with any of the men who obviously wanted her, and she had to bite her tongue to keep from saying, "But I'm taken." How could they understand that what she and her husband, although now long gone, had was still more real than anything she had experienced since.

"I love it here," Sarah said, pulling herself from the reverie and breaking their silence. She dipped her fingers into the water, caressing it and explained, "There's loads of cool fish, snails, worms, clams, crabs and marsh plants in these shallows and marshlands." She recited the inhabitants rotely to overcome her sudden urge to cry, remembering so vividly that she could nearly hear his proposal, her tenuous "yes" and feel the embrace that followed. Controlling her emotions, she turned to KB and Maeve and told them, "It's the only 'wildlife refuge' in the National Park System and although it's resilient, it's still so fragile. A lot like us."

She pulled her hand from the water, shook off the nostalgia and remembered her strong husband the firefighter rushing into burning buildings only to cry later if even the household dog had been lost. She knew the pollution from the crazy project off the coast would overwhelm this sanctuary and explained to a shivering Maeve and distracted KB, "This is where life begins."

The gentle slap of soft waves against the hull was her only answer until KB interjected, "Or ends. There are only a few people who'll choose protecting this area over their own creature comforts. We need more people who know about it, who'll advocate for it."

"Sounds like that's part of our ever expanding job description," Maeve told him flatly.

"Right," he answered smiling, "Add, 'Educate people to how cool and interconnected we are with the ocean, with the planet, so they'll fall so in love with the world that they'll sacrifice creature comforts to take care of her.' It's about showing Grounds how the fate of these invertebrates and literal dinosaurs mimics our own. For example," he jumped from the boat into the shallow marshland and bent to pull an oyster from the muck, "We seeded these after Hurricane Sandy." He looked closely at the mollusk, "Not only do they donate themselves as a delicacy on tables across the world, they purify the water and hold the soil. If they go, we're not far behind." He tossed the oyster into the marsh once again and hauled himself back into the boat, his feet dangling off the stern as he dumped the water from his boots.

Maeve shivered as the sun went behind the clouds and asked, "Would my parents be here?"

Sarah started the engine and let KB answer.

"From what we've just seen," KB said, choosing his words wisely, "They'll be out to sea. That fishing enterprise has the energy to draw just about everything towards it. I'd be surprised if they managed to find sanctuary here."

"So what are we doing here?" Maeve nearly cried.

"We're on our way home. I like it here and wanted to stop," Sarah told her.

"I'm glad we stopped. I needed to process, so thanks," KB told Sarah. "Maeve, we're so over our head. All this work and it seems not much has come of it. But you'll see. The pieces will come together."

Maeve wanted to share the vision she'd had under the sea but still wasn't sure. Now KB had confirmed it. Her parents were at sea. She pushed Abigor's calling from her mind before Sarah could read it. But Sarah turned toward Maeve inquisitively.

Maeve was sure she caught something and for a second, she worried Sarah would know what she'd seen. But the moment passed and Sarah only smiled as she started the engine, turned the boat around and told her, "Did you think you'd what, see them? Or they'd jump up to meet you? It's not that simple, unfortunately. Listen, my permanent mooring is on the other side of this bay. Let's go there and make a plan."

Maeve shivered, waiting for KB to answer. When he didn't, she interjected, "We didn't assess the magnitude of the opposition, I guess. Or the ocean. But I had hoped that, yes, they might jump out to meet me. They are my parents after all."

"That, my friend, was wishful thinking. I'll take you to my place and show you some spells I've been working on," Sarah said, steering toward Brooklyn Bay. "I'm pretty adept at seeing the past and there's some not so ancient history that may help us."

Maeve closed her eyes as the boat sped forward and wondered who was more likely to truly help her, the pirate Abigor or KB and Sarah. She prayed Sarah's gifts would at least help them find her parents' whereabouts and she chastised herself for even thinking of working with the pirate. Her parents would never approve of her crossing that line. Or would they? Had they? Her head hurt weighing options. Had her moral compass been affected by the magnetism from that immense boat? Pushing Abigor's image from her mind, she decided to stick with KB and Sarah. At least until she found her parents. The magic to reassemble them would come, she was sure.

Chapter 10

The boat slowed as they entered Brooklyn Bay and Sarah called to KB who was perched on the bow, ready to pick up her mooring, "It's that one, with the pink stripe," pointing to a mooring marker just off their starboard bow as she slowly maneuvered into the harbor.

"I should have known," KB said with a grin as he leaned off the side of the boat to grab the mooring ball, hauled it onto the deck and tied the cleat before pulling off random pieces of seaweed. Maeve and Sarah both noticed he'd abandoned the sadness she saw overtake him in Jamaica Bay. Relieved, Sarah called to him, "Pink is the color of the divine, by the way."

Wiping his hands on his pants, he walked to the stern and joked, "And all this time I thought it was just for girls."

Each lost in their own thoughts, they trimmed the boat, letting the mundane tasks occupy their minds. Maeve managed the lines, rolling them into neat circles as Sarah stowed gear below. KB swabbed the deck before they gingerly stepped into the small dingy that had been waiting. "Don't rock the boat," Sarah teased, "We've had enough action for today." They cast off with Maeve in the bow, KB rowed and Sarah directed him from the stern toward the shore at Sheepshead Bay where they finally tied up at a small dock full of colorful differently sized dinghies.

They took the little gear they had and walked the ramp toward shore, the floats moving under them and the ramp creaking as they climbed the steepness from low tide. "That's my pick up, over there," Sarah said and pointed to a small white pickup with more than a few dents and rust spots. "It's good transport," she defended, "that's all I need."

"Stop reading my mind," KB said walking towards the truck.

Sarah laughed, hoisted the gear into the back and told them, "It's open," as she pulled herself into the driver seat, started the engine and said to KB with a smirk, "Just like you left your thoughts."

They drove around the dock area of this coastal community in the shadow of Manhattan before they pulled into the drive of a modest house with a small, well-manicured front yard. "There's a backyard as well. I know it's fill, but I love my little private space," Sarah told them, pulling the words from Maeve's mind before she could say them.

As she put the key in the lock and invited them in, Maeve joked, "You ever let people comment for themselves or do you continuously pull random thoughts from people's minds?"

Sarah shrugged, "You wouldn't have the courage to say it, admit that at least." Then she directed her, "Have a hot shower. It'll take the chill off. The bathroom's down there on the right."

"Thanks," Maeve said and left them in the kitchen.

Sarah watched her walk away and asked KB, "So, what do you think of her? She's the one the sisters had been waiting for, right? To save the world? Put the Lights back into the circle of influence?"

"They seem to think so. But she's fresh, new," he hesitated and continued, "a great asset or a huge liability. They're taking a risk. Hell, we're taking the risk. But she's got the purity for sure. Sometimes naivete works in your favor."

"She's got abilities," Sarah emphasized and continued, "But we don't have years to train her in the old ways. The magic is dying and it's not all about feats of physical prowess. She lacks some intuition and understanding the big picture, seeing beyond her own needs. Heck, she's just playing with us while looking for her mom and dad."

"You're right. She lacks depth. But that takes years. She's been on this trajectory what, a few months? And from what we saw today, it'll be on the job training," KB told her, "Why am I telling you this? You know, right?"

"Not everything. I prefer you explain it. Like, tell me more about your plan with that factory?" she demanded referring to KB's project with his sister witch Sadie in the north. "I mean. Seriously, PCB's in housing block?"

KB defended the plan he'd created with his sister but then destroyed with Maeve, "I still think limiting population is the way. I admit that plan was ill founded. But Sadie had lots of rationale behind it. I loved the idea of taking the contaminated material from landfills. If you're so worried about a few side effects for part of the human population, think about the plants and animals. I'd hate to tell you how many 3 eyed frogs I've found in the woods up there. We were basically recycling, containing and minimizing impact."

"That's a one-sided argument. People might say you neglected to look at future generations of people who had to live with those blocks. Sure, reproductive health would be affected, but it might not be the only thing. You've no real idea of the long-term effects."

"Well, I can tell you the effect if the grounds continue on the current trajectory: destruction for the planet. At least the limited number of people would have a place to live. We just got the mix wrong."

Sarah handed KB a hot tea, placed the drone on the table next to him and said, "Getting the mix right should have come first. What about the workers you had?"

"I'm keeping tabs on them, don't worry. It's over. Can we move on with what's in front of us, please?"

"You can't shrug it off like that. They're all connected. The construction, the fish farming and investigation. It's one big cell. And you were involved. Sadie's on their list. She's always defied the council's attempts at controlling things and she grabbed Maeve. Now you've got her. So they could also be looking for you. Especially now that you've got their golden child." Sarah paused to let him take it all in.

When he didn't answer she changed the subject, "You really want Charlotte and Victor to reassemble?"

"Charlotte will find a way and I'd rather be on the side that helps her, if you know what I mean," he answered toying with the drone.

"Good point." She watched him fiddling nervously. Despite the fact that she could read minds and she knew KB since forever, she realized she didn't know him at all. Or at least, she hadn't realized he had changed so much, become so radical. "I can't believe you let Sadie talk you into that project. And for the record, I also can't believe she'll let it go and retire herself to the ether."

KB cut her off, "Who knows. Honestly, I've been over it with a million different scenarios. My head hurts." He needed to work on something new and confided in Sarah, "Listen. Whether Sadie's got other plans or not, we shut that one down. She's been exposed to the council and what happens to my sister next is pretty much out of my hands. I don't need any more lectures. So can we please move on."

"Yes. Of course," Sarah sympathized and knew he was at his limit, patience and commitment wise. She didn't want to push him too far since she knew he might bolt and leave her with Maeve to go it alone. They could manage, but she preferred to have his help. She could barely admit it but, like Maeve, she liked having him around. "Weird," she commented on that feeling, since she'd renounced feeling anything for men since she lost her husband.

"What was that?" KB asked, not understanding.

She smiled and shook her head, "Nothing. Try getting into that drone and see what the more obvious enemy's been up to."

"Tools?"

"Bottom shelf. Over there," she said, pointing toward a large bookshelf in the living room.

KB walked toward the oversized bay window. The

sheer curtains let sunlight filter around him. He closed his eyes, felt the light and breathed in the warmth of the soon to be sunset, letting the guilt and sadness pass. He opened his eyes with a new resolve as he strolled to the bookshelf and grabbed the toolbox. A photo album fell to the floor. He picked it up and, curious, opened it, casually leafing through photos of Sarah's family.

He stopped at one of her in a brides' dress with the groom, amazingly beautiful and happy. The groom's arm rested sensually on her hip and a long white train circled her body creating a cloud like pedestal. He took the album and the toolbox back to the kitchen and said, "Who's the groom? And may I ask what happened?"

Sarah took the album from his hands and gently touched the photo. "I love these pictures. Anyway, Henry was my husband for a little while. One of very few good men," she said nostalgically and then, "He died in 9/11. Firefighter. We were the perfect couple, fire and water."

"Sorry to hear that," he said, secretly relieved that she was currently available. There was something so alluring about Sarah that it made him nearly blush. It wasn't the sort of attraction he'd felt for Marissa in Peru. That had been electric and undeniable, like a rip tide. It had taken them regardless of where they'd wanted to go. This was a deep pull, more subtle and constant. Sarah's story also explained the tragic undertones in all her opinions.

"Yeah. Me too," she said, took a deep breath and continued, "But that was a long time ago. Let's not dwell on a past tragedy while there's another in progress." She wiped a tear from her eye, handed him a sandwich and, as she cradled the album in her arms, opened the tool box and commanded, "Focus."

KB took a bite, mumbled, "Amazing sandwich," and began dismantling the drone. "There's a chip in here somewhere," he said as he turned a tiny screwdriver into tiny screws. "If we can get at it, we can download what's on it."

Chapter 11

Maeve came in and sat down as Sarah put a sandwich in front of her. "Thanks. Can't believe I'm hungry again," she said and continued with a mouth full, "You don't think they put some sort of sabotage device or something in there thinking it may fall into someone's lap?"

KB stopped. "Yeah, I thought about that. But it's a very basic model mostly used to track people around the site. I'm not even sure there's much memory, if any. It's like one of those regularly mounted cameras that downloads to a phone or computer. But we'll see," The last screw fell out onto the table and he smiled, "Voila," as he opened the device and took out a chip. Sarah sat to eat as KB worked between bites. "This piece may have something. Computer?"

Sarah nodded. "In the library just off the living room." "Passwords?" KB asked.

"I'll get you in. No one gets my password," Sarah told him. "Good policy," KB agreed.

They walked to the study, sandwiches in hand. Sarah set him up on the computer saying, "Work away."

She found Maeve standing by the back door looking tired and melancholic as she asked, "OK if I sit out on the deck?"

Sarah nodded, "I'll be out in a bit."

Maeve sat on the chaise with her face to the setting sun, closed her eyes and melted into her fatigue. It was as if all the weight of the world had settled onto her shoulders.

She didn't even have the energy to cry.

Sarah sensed what she was feeling. But before she could mention that she knew it was all connected, KB called from inside, "Come see this. I think I found something." There were small bits and pieces of the drone all over the table. The computer screen showed some blurry video clips.

"I'm not sure it's the only thing this little guy filmed but it looks like it was stationed over that specific area of the hole, umbilical cord or however you want to call it." He moved the video fast forward saying, "I've been over this just once but it appears that harvesting boats come in there with catch to place in the pens. There's one now. See it? It's blurry."

He pointed to a spot on the screen.

"But that's strange because for salmon farming they'd never get the haul from the harbor. They'd have to go far away," Sarah said.

KB froze the frame. "See that boat? It can go pretty far and if you notice there are divers on board as well as huge nets. It's not the way to harvest salmon, that's for sure. They're on something else."

"But we saw them seeding fish," Maeve reminded him, "On the TV, remember?" She didn't want to interrupt to ask how this would help them find her parents so she feigned interest. But she was frustrated at what seemed their lack of concern for her priorities. After all, she'd retrieved the drone. If she hadn't, they'd have no idea what was really happening out there. She guarded her thoughts, however, in case Sarah would read her mind.

He mumbled, "Must have been a side business 'cause this has nothing to do with that."

Sarah moved closer to the screen, squinting to see, "Whatever it is, they take their time. They have rebreathers on the boat, look." She pointed to the divers' equipment and continued, "Those recycle the divers' oxygen so they can stay down longer. They still need to decompress if they go deep but they don't have to bring extra tanks. Makes them lighter. More efficient."

"Sounds horrible for your lungs" Maeve commented.

"That research is still out." Sarah said, "But what would they get deeper?"

KB hit the play button and the three focused, until Sarah said, "Stop. Go back a second and take a look. Yes, right there. Can you make that bigger? Just there." She pointed to a place on the screen where there was a large aquarium sized pen. They could barely see inside. The footage was blurry, "They've got something big in there."

Maeve squinted at the frame, "Looks like an octopus."

They looked more closely, "It's hard to be certain," KB said, "But yeah. That's it."

"What would they do with that?" Maeve asked

"Experiment," Sarah said sadly as she continued, "Did you know the North Atlantic octopus has the largest brain of any invertebrate and a whopping three-fifths of its neurons are located in its tentacles. If we could turn all the animals into humans to take an IQ test, octopi would outscore most, in math anyway, at genius level above 140."

"Wow," KB said, "Einstein was 160," he paused.

"You think they want to learn from them? I'm not sure. I mean, what would the profit motive be? Remember who you're working with here. The Shadows want to control, not help, humanity."

"It's a fine line, right?" Sarah said. "If you know what makes the most basic octopus smart, you can increase your intelligence rather than the entire community. Or you create the enzyme or medicine that does and sell it. It's what big pharma is all about."

"Could be," KB said and then, "Could be even simpler. Lots of people eat octopus. Especially people from places where octopus live closer to the surface and are easier to catch. Maybe they want to farm them."

"Sounds about right. Putting one of the most intelligent species on the planet in a cage so you can eat them," Maeve commented.

"Sick," Sarah sighed. "Whatever they want to do with that poor thing, I'm fairly certain it's not to its benefit."

"Or to ours," KB commented. "Understanding the workings of an intelligent brain from a Shadow perspective is more about control than the common good."

The moment he finished his sentence, the lights flickered and went out. Without light, the sunset gave the house a rose hue that reflected against a dark storm cloud coming in from the harbor. It was beautiful but spooky at the same time.

"This pink doesn't seem so divine," KB commented.

"That's weird," Sarah said pulling back the window curtains, "We're the only house that lost power."

"You have a breaker box?" KB asked, looking past the darkness in Sarah's house at the other houses on the street, all with light. "I can check it."

Sarah grabbed a flashlight from her kitchen drawer and they went to the basement.

"That's it," KB said. "Something switched the breaker. We'll just flip that up." As he did so a bolt of electricity sent him flying back into the wall behind him. The lights flickered back on as KB pulled himself to a seated position on the floor. "Someone's been messing with your box."

"That's impossible," Sarah said in disbelief.

"Nothing is," KB replied, putting his hand on his forehead.

Maeve called from the top of the stairs, "You might want to come up and see this." As she did there was a knock on the door. "Sarah," Maeve called as she peeked through the window to see an elderly woman with a small dog.

Sarah ran up as KB struggled to his feet and climbed the stairs slowly, holding the banister for balance.

"I didn't want to answer in case, well, I'm not sure. But I didn't want to answer her."

Sarah pushed past her saying, "It's ok. You did the right thing. Help KB. I'll take care of the door."

She opened it and greeted the woman warmly, "Hey Mabel. Been awhile."

"Hello Sarah. Are you ok here? You know I saw that your lights all went out and I heard that near explosion. It seemed to come from here. Everything alright?"

"You are so kind to check. But you know, yes, I'm fine. I just had a breaker go."

"Want me to send Ben over to check it? You know he's a wiz at electrical stuff."

From the corner of her eye, Sarah could see Maeve helping KB onto the back porch. When she turned around to tell her neighbor, "I'm fine," she noticed small black dots in the sky. Drones. Maeve was showing KB the same thing out back. "I so appreciate the offer, Mabel. But I've got this one. Thanks," she told her neighbor as she started to close the door.

But Mabel put her foot in the landing to stop her and said, more forcefully than was her nature, "Don't forget, we can help you if you need it. You've been stranger than normal lately Sarah. I worry about you. You know, I have a gentleman friend I think you should meet. It's past time. You can't mourn forever."

Sarah smiled and said, "Seriously Mabel, I have to go and it's not time for me to meet anyone. Henry was my one and only. Thank you."

The woman slowly turned and walked down the stairs calling behind her, "Life is easier with a man in the house." By the time she could turn to say, "You'll see," Sarah had closed the door and was on the back porch with KB and Maeve looking at the small black flying objects circling relatively high in the distance. If you weren't paying attention you'd miss them. But once you saw one, you noticed them all.

"Drones again," Maeve said flatly, "They're looking

for their bro. There's a locator or something on that thing."

"We need to get rid of it. Fast," Sarah said. "We got about everything we can off it, right?"

KB nodded and continued, "They know something's up."

"Well, I'm going to take them from here. They're not going to mess with my box," Sarah said running inside. She scooped all the pieces into a bag and checked to see that Mabel was home before she ordered, "Maeve, come with me. KB, stay here and keep those things away. Cloak the house. Now."

They raced to the dock in the pickup and Sarah jumped into the dingy. But Maeve grabbed the bag of parts and called over her shoulder, "I'll dump it. Remember, I have water skills," as she dove in.

Sarah called after her, "As far as you can."

Maeve dolphin-kicked into the water clutching the bag to her chest. The cold took her breath away but as she worked to move faster, she didn't feel it. She was out of the bay in seconds. Like a turbo charged dolphin, she moved rapidly to a place outside the channel and near where they'd shot the drone down. When she knew she was close, she found a green channel marker and emptied the bag onto it. "I'd hate to litter," she said to the pieces, "So I hope your parents come get you soon."

She pushed the bag into her pants and ducked under the waves to head back. As she did, she saw the light she'd seen the first time she fell in. It seemed farther away, deeper in the ocean. She hovered for a moment in case she could find the container they'd seen in the drone footage. It was there and she dove to find the light. Her ears hurt but she cleared them, took another kick to go farther and saw the animal inside: an octopus. He wasn't panicking, rather he was exploring the too small cage. Her chest tightened for lack of air and she swung her body around to go up.

As she tucked her chin, she connected with the animal, eye to eye and paused, feeling his confusion. When the burning in her chest forced her to release his gaze and surface, another face appeared over it for a nanosecond with dark hair that mimicked the octopus' tentacles framing the scarred face and too white teeth. Abigor again. Couldn't he leave her alone?

"I'm here when you need me," the voice coaxed inside her head.

"Just leave me alone," she thought. Tired of his games and wondering if he were more like the wizard of Oz than a powerful warlock. "All show," she thought and reached toward a tentacle of black hair that was undulating toward her. As she did so, the vision disappeared and her lungs demanded she surface. "I knew it," she told herself as she breached with a mammoth inhale, marked the location with the new star overhead. She promised, "I'll be back," before she swam home, feeling confident she'd chosen the right people to work with and believing – incorrectly it would turn out – that Abigor was more show than substance.

Chapter 12

Sarah was waiting on the dock. "They've moved out. Good job," she told the shivering Maeve. "Let's get back and check on KB."

He met them at the driveway, apologizing, "I'm not sure how I missed a tracker. I didn't find a thing."

"At least we got it away from here. But what about that electricity? How could anyone have tampered with that box?" Sarah asked

"It doesn't make sense unless it was an overload of pure energy. You know sometimes our energy circulates and can get stuck in spaces. When you don't keep your energy in, it lashes out in strange ways." He asked Maeve, "Hey, how've you been feeling, since we came back."

Maeve, still exhilarated from her interaction below the sea yet not wanting to share or even think about it in case Sarah would read her mind, merely answered, "Right now? I feel good. Concerned about what I saw down there but good. And a little cold, honestly."

"Have a shower, Maeve. Mi casa es tuya," Sarah told her.

"Before you go," KB caught her and asked, "How were you feeling before the adrenalin kicked in to get rid of the drone. Were you sad?" KB asked.

Shivering, Maeve stuttered, "Actually, yes, but more disgusted. I feel for the animals. So, I'm more angry than sad. And frustrated by our lack of progress to find my parents. To do anything of substance, really." She sighed, "I guess planning isn't my forte," and went inside.

KB spoke to Sarah as they followed her in, "You know, that could be it. We need to check her energy body. I've only been working with the physical and she's got speed, intuition, amazing sensory powers of smell, sight and taste. But perhaps she's got internal energy surges and leaks. She needs to learn to use that wisely and keep them all in check. Her anger and sadness could have accumulated and caused the short. It was still collecting behind the break even when the lights were out. That's what threw me across the room."

"Seriously?" Sarah asked incredulously.

"Totally. We all have these energy channels. Wisdom traditions label them as meridians, nadis, chakras. But some are stronger than others. The sisters gave her some amazing tools and she had some latent powers that they stirred to life when they did. But they didn't have time to help her learn their nuances, like dealing with them before they explode. We'll help her figure it out. She'll need to learn to control it. But there's no other explanation I know for that shock," KB said, still weak from the incident.

"Wow. She's got some power then. I've never had that happen, You?" Sarah mused.

"Before my war, yeah. I'd leak every so often and things would get ugly. I nearly started a gang war once that way, working in Harlem. But since then, I've learned control and I'm not that person any longer. I don't care as much as she does," he said nostalgically.

"You talk about control and maturity like it's a bad thing, KB. I would say, you've evolved," Sarah told him sympathetically and put her hand on his.

"You could say that," he replied unenthusiastically but squeezed her hand before he let go and continued, "You could also say I've been jaded and I'm not willing to risk it all for the good of the Grounds. The planet will survive with or without them. After working with Sadie, I'm done with trying to change their downward spiral. It's nearly impossible anyway. All Sadie's work, centuries of caring and healing and the council is all over her after the episode with the bricks. Everyone who's touched her will be implicated. That means her sisters, Maeve, me, now you too," he drifted. "Imagine her father tried to send us both into that abyss of space in the center of the earth! Our mother saved us but got carried along with him."

Sarah interrupted, asking, "Wait. You and Maeve are related?"

"Maternally. From generations ago. I'm an older soul than Maeve. But yes, Charlotte's most recent spawn is Maeve."

Sarah raised an eyebrow but said nothing since Maeve wandered back. KB nodded and asked, "You ok?"

"I'm beat but hungry, again. Could we call for pizza? In New York they deliver by drone." KB and Sarah laughed. Then Maeve joined and they couldn't stop until the delivery guy knocked on the door.

Taking the last slice, Maeve confided, "They're working on something deep in the ocean," They were on the back porch and a cool breeze gently crossed the rooftops and trees around them before it caressed their skin. KB wiped tomato sauce from his chin and paid attention as Sarah asked, "What'd you see?"

"Returning the pieces of the drone," she explained, "There was this glow from deep down," she paused. "I felt them. From that far away. Pure Shadow. That's twice now."

Sarah said, "Really?"

Maeve continued, "Yeah, remember when I fell in? I saw it that time as well. And I felt the pull. A sick, seductive drawing you in." She finally decided they were safe and was dying to tell someone. So she continued, "And there was a vision. The same guy from the ship, scarred face, seductive smile. He was calling me. It was Abigor."

Sarah's eyes widened and her jaw dropped as she leaned closer to Maeve and nearly shouted, "What?"

"He was there? In the sea? That deep?" KB questioned her.

Maeve nodded and answered, "Well, it was more of a vision, a sort of projection of his face into the water. He was floating over the crate and yes, it's what we thought: an octopus."

"What did he say? Why didn't you tell us sooner?" KB stuttered.

"I wasn't sure about any of it. He told me he could bring me to my parents. I so wanted to believe him I nearly followed his image back to the boat. And it wasn't the first time. He's been pretty much a vision stalker," she confided, "jumping into my space since we left West Point."

Neither KB nor Sarah spoke. Both were thinking the same thing: Abigor was after Maeve and wouldn't stop. It wasn't the drone he was looking for just then, it was her.

And now he'd seen how capable she was.

"But I didn't," Maeve interjected and broke the silence. "I know he's evil and it would be so wrong. And I didn't tell you sooner because, honestly? I was tempted to take his help. Working with you guys is taking so long." She paused to breathe and take in what she'd finally said out loud: she'd been willing to compromise the entire planet to get what she wanted.

"Well," KB said, "You might find your parents, but you'd lose yourself. Your call." "KB's right," Sarah said, "that's a one way street once you take it."

KB studied Maeve's face across the table, surprised that his brother would be so bold and so powerful to follow her in vision. A nervous pit formed in his belly at even the thought of confronting Abigor, ruthless sociopath that he was. Finally, KB said, "Listen, I know things aren't going as fast as you'd hoped. But we're close. Now more than ever. We know our mom and your dad are on his ship. In what form, we'll have to see. But it's all connected. That's huge."

"I know. But I can't believe they haven't contacted me. They can't be in human form yet. If they were, I know they'd find me. I mean, It wasn't like we had a small argument. That was a fight to the near death." Maeve was hurting. She could feel the touch of her mother's hand in hers. She missed her so much and it didn't make sense that if they were in fact with this mad pirate, Charlotte didn't reach out to Maeve. Could they still be angry? Embarrassed that now Maeve knew their story? Afraid that she might still be angry and was now so powerful she could retaliate?

The ideas raced through her mind. But, no. They would never hold a grudge. She remembered them at dinner, laughing, her dad making fun out of something. Sure, Charlotte was more distant emotionally than Victor but she was also so much more present in the day to day. Maeve had great memories of polishing nails together, shopping trips, Charlotte took Maeve with her on her volunteer visits to schools and nursing homes. They were girlfriends as much as mother daughter.

And there was that time on their way to Lincoln Center when a guy on the subway tried to grope Maeve. Charlotte confronted him and literally pushed him off the train. At the time, Maeve had no idea how she'd done it. She'd only said, "You need help, pervert," and forced him to the door by walking continuously toward him, pushing him with her mere presence. When the door slid open at the next stop, he literally fell off the train. Charlotte came back and put her arm around her daughter and said, "Don't ever think that was your fault." It felt so good to be protected.

It didn't matter if Charlotte didn't always interact like Victor did with long drives, boat trips or hikes in the woods. She'd rarely join them, saying she needed her down time. More complicated than Maeve's dad, Charlotte took time for herself. But she also sacrificed most of her life for Maeve's and Maeve knew, if Charlotte had reassembled, she'd be looking for her daughter.

KB realized she was struggling to understand. But he saw the other facets of Charlotte, her ambiguity and willingness to allow things to fall so they could rebuild. He'd been the victim of her lack of maternal instinct and knew Charlotte would choose Charlotte over even her children every time. KB remembered the time Charlotte was up for review with the council the same day KB was finishing a harrowing martial arts test by battling his brother. She went to her review without even mentioning she'd not be there to see her sons fight or to help them navigate the complicated emotional fallout afterwards. That slight and many others like it had fueled the brothers' long standing inability to even talk to each other.

He also knew how much Charlotte loved Abigor. And if it was even equal to how she loved Maeve, she'd want to keep her daughter out of this. She certainly wouldn't be jumping from the water to drag Maeve into it all. He took Maeve's hand. "We'll figure it all out. But we know taking that ship means finding your parents. So there's no more questioning, no more feeling like you're doing the wrong thing. Our goals have certainly aligned. Although I have to admit, I'm surprised you didn't trust us and tell us sooner. But I respect you for weighing your options."

"They're my parents, KB. I'll do what it takes to find them. Even if it means not working with you." There. She'd said it. She could go this alone if she had to.

"I get it," he told her, "But you're not ready yet. Whether you believe it or not, you need us. So, now tell us more about what you saw down there, besides Abigor."

She decided not to argue the point, uncertain if he were right. Instead of debating her strengths, she related what she'd witnessed below the surface. "Well, it was bizarre. They had an octopus in that crate. You were right, Sarah. But, he didn't seem to panic. He was exploring the crate, nothing more."

Sarah hated even thinking Abigor wanted Maeve. Was she so powerful that even this evil pirate needed her? She pushed the idea into the recesses of her mind where the pain of having lost her husband to Abigor's evil lived vibrantly. The Shadows were behind the attack on the World Trade Center and Abigor was their most involved. "Show them fear. They'll be easier to control. These American Grounds are too free," she'd heard him tell the Shadow Council at a meeting she'd snuck into with Samuel just before the attack. She'd watched in a strange combination of fascination and repulsion as he told the Shadows, "Perhaps we can't educate them but we can control them. That, my friends, is the way to take over."

She and Samuel had been discovered and had run from the place before they learned more details. But she'd experienced a sick feeling when her husband rushed to the world trade center. She hoped it was only the magnitude of the attack. But no, it was her intuition that the love of her life wouldn't come back. Avenging him may not change anything. "But it might change the future," a voice deep in her heart told her.

So she'd swallow this latest insult that Maeve didn't trust her until it could become a greater strength and, in the right moment, she'd avenge her husband and rid the world of that monster Abigor. When she could finally speak, she merely said, "Bizarre. North Atlantic Octopus generally live deeper, 200 to 600 meters, nearly 2000 feet. The water temperature at that depth is about 40 degrees Fahrenheit. There's no way you were that deep and that's a nearly impossible depth and climate to maintain a lab."

"Not necessarily," KB said. "Not if it's a submarine that goes down and slowly comes up, pressurized, taking a few days below before surfacing. Or unmanned, pure robotics and It could fit in one of those ships' hulls." He shook his head, as if it were all too much and added, "There's a lot going on."`

"The light was powerful, visible from not so deep. Perhaps they want to see if the octopus can survive at higher levels? But why octopus?" Maeve asked. "And why here in the North Atlantic? There are octopus in climates and places way more accessible. I don't get it."

KB continued, "The 'why octopus' is easy. They're amazingly intelligent beings. I mean, octopuses have 3 hearts. It's so cool. Two pump blood to the gills and a larger heart circulates blood to the rest of the body. They have 9 brains because, in addition to the central brain, each of the 8 arms has a mini-brain that allows it to act independently. And, they are marketable as food. Bummer in my opinion, but they're popular in the city. A delicacy in many cultures."

"So there's lots to research and sell afterwards," Sarah commented. "But Maeve's comment is a good one. Why here? It's a harsh climate."

"Harder to discover their project, perhaps," Maeve said thoughtfully, "That could be the why. I mean, it's US waters, not international. They're amazingly close to shore for a big operation so they're cloaking well. They're deep enough so no one would casually find them. Very few people are fishing that species here since this work in deep, cold water takes time and money."

KB commented, "Grounds won't search the perpetrators out. They don't care enough."

"I think they'd care if they understood. They're too removed. But we care more than enough," Sarah confidently told him, "and regardless what they're up to, we'll take them down."

"But how?" KB said. "It's walking into their hands from above. They're not nice people. And from below, the depth puts us all at risk."

Sarah agreed, "We'll need allies and facts. So far we have only hunches. How can we get a real sense of what's going on?"

"Above? Drones," Maeve stated and then continued. "We could infiltrate their drones with one of ours. They won't notice one more. We'd need it there for what, a weekend?"

"Not even," KB mused. "The model they're using isn't uncommon. What is, is its ability to process info and not store it. So they get a constant stream of intel to monitor. But they have no history. So they're really just for security."

"Living in the moment," Sarah sighed "But if we're using them for less time, couldn't we store information? On one we can buy anywhere?"

KB nodded saying, "OK. So that's the above. Below?

We definitely need some help."

Maeve groaned inwardly, wishing she had accepted Abigor's offer. She was so tired of all these delays. She also found him more and more seductive. The roughness, his ability to give her what she wanted, his power, she honestly couldn't get him out of her mind.

Sarah read her thoughts and offered quickly, "We could visit my old professor at Princeton who's been studying marine life for ages. He may be able to help. Let's visit him and get a drone in the air. Regardless of what they're doing under the sea, they've got to come up at some point."

"We can modify a commercial one," KB said. "Where can we check those out? I'd like to study one especially if we're asking your PhD friend about it. I'd rather not waste his time." What he was thinking was more that he didn't want to look like an idiot, least of all in front of these two women he was having trouble keeping up with mentally and physically.

"He'll be happy to see us, trust me," Sarah answered him. "He and I have a connection," she winked at Maeve and smiled before continuing, "There's Costco off the highway. We can buy one and KB, you can study it on the drive to Charles."

"And I can ask him about the chemistry of reassembling my parents. Think he'd have some ideas?" Maeve asked, relieved to have confided her secret with them and more confident now they'd make progress.

"He probably will," Sarah agreed. "Although it's not

marine science, he is amazing with marine magic." She grabbed her keys, "Let's go. It's still not that late. I'll ring Charles to tell him we're coming."

Chapter 13

"We'll take the scenic route," Sarah called as she locked the front door and skipped down her porch stairs. "Through Forest Park to the State Park, then along the coast. There shouldn't be too much traffic and it isn't far. They built that mammoth superstore right on an inlet by the harbor."

"I've never understood Grounds' inability to see beauty in nature, even if it's damaged. It can always come back," Maeve mused. As she hoisted herself into the pickup, she remembered the drives she'd take with her father. He loved the scenic route. They'd often head north on Merritt Parkway rather than use the interstate. She loved how he'd make fun of the satellite trees created to mimic real trees but were actually satellite towers. She laughed thinking of his discourse about how ridiculous it looked. When they'd drive Riverside drive, cars would honk as her father slowed for the amazing views. They'd often stop in the small parks that dotted the graceful curves of the parkway. He loved the winding road and often played music from a list of country songs called "Dangerous Curves".

Sarah turned toward her, feeling Maeve's nostalgia and reading her mind that on those drives she felt like the only one in his world. She realized that Maeve so missed being that special someone.

"They're damaged. That's why," KB called from the back seat interrupting their reverie. "And they don't want to come back. They like things the way they are: convenient. It reflects directly onto everything in their lives."

No one could disagree as Sarah drove highway 678, sped through the parks and finally turned toward the airport along the coastal community that ran directly into the mammoth superstore. Pulling into the parking lot, they could see Rockaway Beach.

"I'll get food while you're in the technical section. It's just as you enter. If we don't make a plan we'll be here all day. It's distracting."

"That's their plan," KB commented dryly. "You buy more stuff."

Sarah showed her membership card at the door and KB told Maeve, "You might want to help Sarah. That way you can get foods you like. You seem to be the one who's always hungry." He wanted to be alone for a while but didn't know how to come out and say it. The constant company was draining and he wanted to ask the clerk questions uninhibited. Feeling as if he needed to know everything was exhausting him.

But Maeve was adamant, "I'll go with you. I trust Sarah with the food." "And you don't trust me with the drones?" KB asked her.

"It's not that, I'd like to learn about them. Two heads are better than one, no?" "Not always," KB mumbled as Maeve followed him to the electronics. KB asked the young man organizing cables, "You guys carry drones?"

"Sure. The models we have are over here," he said and walked them toward the display asking, "Have any idea what you'd like?"

"Something with storage capacity for a 3-day period."

"Hmm. That's difficult," he said, perusing the case and explaining, "These could send you footage while hovering but not for that long. The flight battery is 12 hours max. You want them for security?"

"Something like that," Maeve answered.

KB interjected, "Can we see what you've got?" wanting to take control of the conversation.

"Sure thing," the young man explained how drones can be controlled remotely as he put two on the display case. "You can use your smartphone or tablet and the wireless connectivity lets you view the drone and its surroundings from a birds-eye perspective. You can also leverage apps that pre-program specific GPS coordinates and create automated flight paths. Another handy wireless feature is tracking battery charge. You'll know when she needs to come home."

KB held one up, examining it and said, "Joystick and GPS. Ha. These are like playing a video game."

He chuckled but the salesman added, "Yeah. But behind this easy user interface, there's an accelerometer, a gyroscope and other complex technologies working to make the mechanics of drone flight as smooth as possible. It's a little wireless technology and a whole lot of physics. Pretty amazing."

Maeve nodded agreement and said, "And you can bug the crap out of people around you."

KB smiled and told the salesman, "We'll take both models," and then to Maeve, "I'll study these."

Maeve asked, "How much are these things?"

The salesman reached below the display counter and

said, "These are higher end, semi- professional. Let's see," he mumbled as he looked at the price. "This one at $529 and the other at $749," and continued, "You can get cheaper at Walmart for sure or Sam's even but they won't have this level of function."

"Thanks," KB acknowledged, "These are good." The clerk handed him two cards with the images and models telling them, "You take these and I'll meet you at checkout with the items.

"Right," Maeve agreed, "I can't wait to see how you pay for these babies."

KB smiled and scolded, "Watch that negative self-talk will you? It's interfering with my manifestation."

Sarah was in line already and waved to them to join, asking, "How'd it go?" KB responded by flipping the cards at her, "We've got two I'd like to study." "They're pricey, however," Maeve interjected.

"Yeah," KB said, "A little more than a grand for the two of them."

Sarah laughed and said, "That's so funny. I have a credit from a returned snow blower for just about that much. They wouldn't give me money back since I'd used it. Between those and the food, we should get about 10 dollars change."

KB smugly looked at Maeve. "Magic."

She smiled and shook her head as the clerk gave the two drones to the checkout person. KB continued, "Seriously, you need to see it if you want it. Abundance is all around. You can have what you want. And we need the magic to continue so, believe and be grateful."

Chapter 14

As they shopped drones in Costco, a white sedan drove slowly past Sarah's house and stopped on the other side of the street. Kevin opened the passenger side door and stood, stretching and complaining, "These rental cars. I can't believe you totaled ours back in Jersey."

Mark struggled to open his telescoping cane and shifted from behind the steering wheel to exit saying, "Not my fault," guiltily as he leaned into the cane and touched his leg where the oozing wound came through his pants still.

"Not what the police decided. Or that bitch," Kevin commented and pulled his pants up to adjust the ever-present pistol he kept tucked into them. He slammed the door as a plane flew loudly overhead.

Mark retorted over the din, "It may have gone differently if you'd learn when to shut your mouth." He continued, "For now, let's look for that white pickup, remember? And anything that says they're here. I'd like to get rid of that kid and get Andrew off our back once and for all. He won't rest 'til he knows she's out of the picture. Why he cares so much is beyond me."

"Could it be that she'll cost the Sheriff jail time if she ever leaks those papers she's stashed from the site?" Kevin mocked his boss as he limped slowly down the street, leaning into the cane he'd come to depend on and wondering why the old Sheriff wanted Maeve dead. He didn't understand that

Andrew still hoped to revive the plan he and Sadie had worked on to limit human population. It wasn't as if Andrew cared so much about the world. But he cared about having contact with his ex-lover. Having even a business connection with Sadie gave him hope she'd be there for him. Andrew couldn't accept the council was sending her into the ether and he blamed Maeve for all of it.

Mark sniffed the air as he limped across the street and commented to Kevin, "They've been around. I can smell it."

"Well smell where so we can get this over with," Kevin told him. "The longer we're on the street the more people might see us. They have contacts all over this neighborhood."

"Yeah," Mark mused as he passed Sarah's house and stopped, leaning on his cane and mumbling, "So do we." He stayed there a moment, looking into the window and still sniffing the air when the neighbor walked from her home with a small white terrier. As they turned toward the men her dog started to bark, baring his teeth and pulling on the leash.

"Sorry," she apologized as she struggled to keep him from attacking Mark. She forced a smile as she pulled the ferocious small dog away saying, "He's usually so friendly." The dog kept barking as she pulled him down the block saying, "Gabi, calm down." Exasperated, she finally picked him up and carried him out of sight and smell of the two.

"Let's go," Mark finally decided. "This is where they were but they're not here now. We're late," he glared at Kevin and continued. "Sooner or later we'll catch up with them. I've a hunch where they're headed. We'll make one stop on the way."

The two glumly crossed the street, got back in the car and drove away, Kevin's disappointed bandaged face in the passenger side window looking toward the house as the neighbor returned with her dog, now barking at the car. The owner calmed the pup down saying, "They're leaving Gabi, you can quiet down now." She made a mental note of the license plate on her phone before she stood and sent the number to her neighbor.

Chapter 15

They left the mega store satisfied with all they'd bought and loaded the car. KB sat in the back seat reading drone manuals. As Sarah backed out of the parking space, she felt a bump and heard a grind of metal on metal. "Shit. I didn't see anyone coming," she cursed and got out of the car to see what had happened.

KB closed the boxes. "Wait here. We'll handle this." He sensed an undercurrent of deceit in the air as opened the door. Looking behind them and remembering the accident from in front of the diner, he cautiously told Maeve, "Practice your cloaking will you? You can't be too careful out here."

Maeve slouched in the seat and chanted her cloaking mantra as she sparkled into invisibility. Sarah examined her fender and that of the white sedan she had barely scratched. The driver's door opened and two polished shoes floated over the pavement.

"It's barely a scratch," she mumbled. When she turned to confront the driver she exclaimed, "Samuel! What are you doing here?" She read his mind and realized he was looking for Maeve.

"I let you in for that one," he told her with a smile as he gave her a hug. But she wondered why he'd come all this way to find the young woman he'd just seen at his diner. She couldn't discern an answer and realized he was blocking her.

"KB," Samuel called, "This must be a record, twice in one day. Actually, twice this decade." The two embraced and

Samuel asked for Maeve as she sparkled back to visibility once she heard him. Samuel said, "You're getting better at that, for sure," as she walked toward him.

"We've been working with her a bit," KB told him and then, "How'd you find us here? Wouldn't it have been easier to call?"

"Ha," Samuel told him, "Too bad you only use your burners. But I never intended for you to back into me."

Sarah frowned, "I really didn't see you coming. I bet your cloaking skills hid the entire car."

"Could be," Samuel said. "But it's only a scratch. So what's going on? Where are you all headed?" he peered into the back seat and said, "With drones?"

"Come on Samuel," Sarah answered him, "I know you've been monitoring us. Who are you kidding? And you'd have been more help if you'd showed up when those Shadow drones came by. That was fireworks for sure."

Well, yes," he answered. "I have been peeking now and again and it looks like you're in deeper than we thought, or hoped." Samuel winked at Maeve, "Excuse the pun." He paused for only a second and explained, "I thought you could use a hand."

Sarah wanted to believe him but felt a certain skepticism that she couldn't shake. KB, excited to see his old friend, wondered why the sudden change of heart. He agreed they were over their heads and loved the idea of another male perspective on the operation. But he couldn't help wondering why Samuel would suddenly want to join them. As an advisor, he rarely got his hands dirty these days. A powerful ally for sure. But most of his work was generally done floating over United Nations meetings trying to influence peace on earth. For him to come to see them, physically, meant something was up. KB needed to know what.

So he asked, "You found us to join the fight? On the ground?"

Samuel measured his words carefully, "Yes. I'd like to help you find and reassemble Charlotte." There he'd said it out loud. His recent desire to unite with her and join their power was out. Realizing Maeve was confused he quickly added, "And Victor, your dad, of course. That goes without saying."

KB was the wiser and commented, "Does it?"

Sarah frowned, skeptical. She knew he and Charlotte had a thing going on. But she saw something more sinister in her friend Samuel. He had a plan that he wasn't sharing with them. And he'd blocked her so she couldn't find out what it might be.

But Maeve was overjoyed. Finally someone with her relatively mundane priority, saving her parents before saving the earth. She ran to him and hugged him around the neck until he hugged her back. When she stepped away, she was happier and more hopeful than ever. "Well, let's go then. Should I drive with you, Samuel?"

KB interjected, "Why not let me go with Samuel and you with Sarah. I could use some male bonding, if you don't mind, Sam."

Sarah was relieved. She and KB were thinking the same thing: something didn't add up. They were both now hesitant to let Maeve alone with Samuel.

Not wanting to be separated, Samuel smiled blandly, "Why don't I leave my car here and we can all go together. One big happy family."

Chapter 16

"He was my professor. Super cool guy. And my thesis advisor, and a Light." Sarah told Maeve with a smile before she turned up Tracey Chapman's Fast Car saying, "I love this song."[1] Sarah wasn't about to divulge that they'd been lovers before she met her husband Henry. And Charles, a married man. It had been a quick, unconscionable affair and Charles should have known better. Sarah was a sophomore and Charles an adjunct professor. But they were both Lights, both working with the council and both lonely. Charles' family lived in Jersey City. The commute was too far so Charles had taken the resident advisor position on Sarah's dorm floor. He lived there most weeknights and went home most weekends. It had been incorrect on so many levels.

Maeve started to sing along as Sarah reminisced. "And I y I had the feeling I could be someone, be someone" as they drove off the interstate and onto the access toward Princeton University. Large trees, Tudor and colonial style houses lined the way to the prestigious university. Maeve wondered if this was where Tracey Chapman would move when she finally got promoted. These suburbs might not be so welcoming to that check out girl.

"Is this where you studied?" Maeve asked, mesmerized. "It's almost nicer than Harvard."

"Almost?" asked Sarah incredulously, "Way nicer. And just as good, if not better. Anyway, yes. I studied here. Marine Studies. Charles was my coastal engineering professor. Amazingly gifted and kind. He's waiting for us."

They parked behind a 3 story red brick building on the main street and the four climbed the stairs, although Samuel had a habit of floating more than walking.

Distractedly Maeve wondered if that was good for his body, not moving much. He gave her a big smile. "I'm past the point of working out. Don't worry about me."

"I didn't mean anything by it. Just wondering." She needed to be careful of her thoughts around these people. "Isn't that a little rude to be reading minds all the time?" she asked herself out loud. "Kind of like looking through someone's sock drawer."

"I'll try to control it," Samuel answered, "But let's stay focused, shall we?"

Maeve didn't love his tone of voice, harsh and nearly an order. Even her father wouldn't use that tone. It was unnerving.

The gang walked to where a tall, academic looking man waited. He was almost a cliché of a professor. He even wore a bow tie. He extended his hand to Sarah first and said softly, in a welcoming voice, "So nice to see you Sarah," putting both his hands around hers. There was an awkwardness that kept them from embracing but if you paid attention you saw they both were resisting that impulse.

"You too, Professor." Sarah locked eyes with him.

"Charles, please," he scolded. "After all we've been through together," he searched her face for some recognition of their affair, but she masked it well. Self-consciously, he released her hands and addressed the group, explaining, "Gosh, we've known each other for years and now Sarah's graduated." He laughed, "Samuel! This must be big to bring you down here." He hugged his old friend and then turned to KB and Maeve saying, "And this dynamic duo. Well, lately you're the talk of the council, in case you didn't know. Mostly good, except for the fact that they are missing Charlotte and rumor has it she sacrificed herself for you guys. That really made the news."

"I'd say she did it mostly for Maeve. Nice to meet you."

"Don't assume anything, KB. That's when you get into trouble. Regardless, she'll come out of it all ok. Charlotte always does."

"I'm certain," KB winked.

Charles regarded him warily. "Come in. Come in. I'm reviewing some undergrad papers, and I'd love a break. What've you got there?"

"Drones," KB placed them on the desk.

Charles examined the machines. "Those are pretty good. Shame they don't have more battery life. It would help you see more." He smiled at KB. "I know why you're here. Sarah sent me some background. We've been monitoring disturbances in the electric currents underwater for a while. Vibrations emanating from either a box they've lowered or some sort of submarine vessel. Regardless, they come to the surface at some point almost every other day. There's no set schedule but we know since the vibrations stop. You'll need to be vigilant to catch them. Good idea on the drones. And when you share the intel with the Council perhaps you'll be back in their graces."

Samuel nodded. "It would be nice to get you back on

board."

"Can you help with battery life, Charles? We need more time," Sarah interrupted, feeling KB's discontent with Samuel's last comment. She knew the last thing on KB's radar was ingratiating himself with the Council, least of all by sharing information about his brother, Abigor. At the end of the day, they were still siblings.

"There's several things you need, actually. Longer battery life is just one of them. Please," he motioned for them to sit, "You need the capacity to withstand strong winds and interference from below. Also, some sort of retrieval mechanism or remote detonator in case they're discovered. You don't want them to know you're watching, right?"

"You've got a point."

"It's all doable," Charles commented optimistically, picking one up. "We need to figure out how, is all."

"What do you think they're studying, professor?" Sarah asked.

"Charles, remember?" he reminded her and moved his hand a little too close to hers on the table. "I've been thinking about that a lot. They want money and control. The ocean bottom is full of specimens we know very little about that could be exploited for economic gain. Take seaweed for example, a wonderful source of vitamins, could be added to so many foods without compromising taste. Also an amazing building material when cured correctly. Then there are the animals. They're not in the deepest of waters but there's marine life worth studying at all levels and most of it moves between depths. There's algae that can be processed into certain medicines too. The list goes on."

"So, best to see what they're up to and extrapolate from there?" KB asked. "What about octopus?" Maeve interjected. "I'm sure I saw one in a cage down there."

"Well, there's a lot to study there for sure," Charles said thoughtfully. "Thought patterns, ability to disguise, camouflage and change color, actual cognizant thought and rational thinking. They're amazing beings. Are you sure that's what you saw?"

"They had one in a crate. I saw him before I needed to surface," she replied.

"You've been swimming?" Charles smiled, amused. "Isn't it a little chilly for that still?"

"You've no idea about our wonder woman here. She's amazing in the water," Samuel said.

Maeve blushed and told them, "It's a long story, but yes. And I saw one that someone was holding in a too small aquarium-like tank. That's why I asked."

Charles nodded. "Well, the best case would be to watch them for a few days and answer some what's and why's. Research is good and the more we know about these environments the better."

"We don't have time. My parents are out there, and they need to be saved. I'd love to get you a research paper, but I need to move on this. We need to move on this," Maeve beseeched them.

"I doubt they are writing a paper to help create a better world, regardless," KB commented.

Charles laughed, "We can only dream. The thing is, until you know, we have nothing. But there may be a way to use the drones to your advantage. There's a guy I know in Coney Island who works with birds. Vincent. He's amazing."

Maeve mumbled, "Another delay, seriously?"

"Let's get this right, remember? The big fight?" KB told her and then asked, "Birds?"

"I've heard of him," Samuel interjected, more interested than ever.

Sarah tried to read his mind but he'd blocked her totally. She watched him carefully for clues to his motives. "We all give ourselves away at some point," she told herself. As she thought that, Charles leaned back in his chair and put one arm on the back of hers. She smiled at his transparency but knew there was no chance in hell she'd go down that road again. There was only one man in her life and he'd died. She was done.

KB picked up on her body language and smiled at the challenge. "Things never change," he thought. "The less interested she is in me, the more I'm interested in her."

Oblivious to the mental gymnastics happening all around him, Charles eased into his closeness with Sarah. "He's a carnival engineer who retired early so to speak, after a roller coaster accident. Now he mostly studies the flight patterns of coastal birds, you know, gulls, osprey and even the cormorant. He's become very connected with them and lives in an old warehouse down there. A bit of a recluse," Charles paused, wondering how Vincent would handle this gang on his doorstep. "The cormorant, you know, is a diver. He may have one or two who could help you to retrieve a drone or even place a camera underwater. You don't have the luxury of moving forward 'til you know more. You've witnessed their power and now they've got you on their radar. You need a strong plan before taking the next step."

"So," Sarah said with a sigh, "we're off to Coney Island. Should we keep the drones?"

"By all means," Charles confirmed, "I'm sure he can modify them to adapt them for underwater. Vince has been studying cormorant feathers and oils for waterproofing. You'll love him. I'll give him a call. I bet he'll see you tonight if you're up for it. You're heading back that way regardless."

"I love Coney Island, a walk on the wild side is always good for the soul," KB said.

"I'd love to go just to meet Vincent. He sounds like someone who can get things done," Maeve commented. She found his story absolutely fascinating and felt a kindred spirit in another engineer. Another dropout from the mainstream as well. Maybe he was the spark that could get them moving.

They could hear Charles talking excitedly on the phone in the next room and when he walked back, he clapped his hands together, "He'll wait for you. I'll draw you a map of the location. I'd rather not send you the GPS since you're being followed, you now know. And not just by Samuel here. But if you bumped into him, you could literally bump into someone not so supportive." He quickly sketched the simple directions and handed it to Sarah saying, "Remember, don't judge a book by its cover, ok? He's amazingly intelligent and accomplished."

Before they could say goodbye, Maeve reminded Charles, "About my parents." She cast a glance at KB and Sarah. "Would you have clues on how to reassemble them?"

KB and Sarah were silent. Charles hesitated but then answered, "Your parents will need the Council's approval before forming again. But there are formulas that will facilitate that relatively easily. You need to find them first, however."

"You know about them?" Maeve asked elated.

"Yes, Maeve. All the coven knows about your parents. They're big news these days," he confided to her. "And the good news is that their molecules can regroup. We know they rode the river out to the ocean, like all things. The not so good news is Abigor recovered them."

Samuel added, "We're not sure if it's willingly or not."

"Well, I know it's not. I mean, my parents have issues, I admit. But they'd never seek that monster, molecularly or physically. Never," Maeve emphasized.

Charles continued, "Maeve, the council's been watching. We, well they, suspect your parents were responsible for Sadie's project, the one with the PCBs. It was under their watch that she managed to create this most damaging scenario. They're holding them responsible and looking to sanction them, perhaps even strip their positions. We, well really again they, since I'm only an advisor not a voting member like Samuel, haven't come to agreement on that issue. So it's not unlikely they'd move toward Abigor. You see, if they reconstitute with him, they're powerful, relatively free and can maintain their hold on the Light council. He knows that so he's also searching for the way to reassemble them. Abigor's a special case, a rogue that the council has used in the past. That's why he's nearly untouchable and the council's sanctions don't cover Abigor's boat. Granted he's in international waters but the council has bypassed the Grounds' laws in the past. Regardless, once they assemble, the collective needs to release them and decide their fate. That means they'd stand trial if they leave the ship in any form. So, they may be there in molecular form hoping Abigor can form them before the council finds them."

Maeve searched Sarah and KB's faces, "Did you guys know this?" She didn't give them time to answer. "I've got to get onto that ship."

"Not alone," Samuel touched her shoulder, "You'll need us. Your father is so ambitious and right now still angry. He's furious at your mother. You know she sacrificed him to save you."

Maeve still dreamt of her mom taking her father into that watery depth while she and KB watched helplessly.

Charles assured her, "Regardless, you'll find them there. Perhaps reassembled but I doubt Abigor has that strength or wisdom. You'll find them first by stopping this crazy project."

Maeve shook her head in disbelief. "How can they hold them responsible for Sadie?"

"They believe your father either knew or should have. They are family after all," Samuel explained.

Angry, Maeve answered him, "And KB's family but I have no idea what he's been up to in the last years. I had no idea he was even alive. And even if I wanted to, I couldn't control him."

Charles answered, choosing his words carefully, "But you're not on the council. You've not accepted that position of oversight and trust. Your parents had."

She held back a scream and the lights in the office flickered as she made fists with both hands.

"Take a deep breath, Maeve," KB counseled. "We can wait this one out."

Charles backed off to the corner of the room and Sarah followed him as a bulb in the overhead light popped. KB stood in front of her and took his hands on her shoulders to hold her down as she levitated off the floor, her face contorted in anger. She tried to push him away but gave up and instead screamed a loud sad moan that vibrated into the furniture and shook everything around. Frames on the walls fell to the floor as she returned to the ground and slumped into a sad ball on the oriental carpet turning her head side to side and hugging herself. KB sat next to her and wrapped his arms around hers. "Patience, Maeve. One step at a time. They'll be ok."

Samuel watched from across the room, keen to see the power in this young protegé. He smiled wryly, clapping his hands. "Well done." He looked at Charles, "Now that is expressing your emotions!"

Charles ignored him but something about Samuel made him curious about his true motives for being there.

Maeve let KB hold her a moment longer, loving his proximity, feeling safe.

KB told Samuel, "Bummer is that she's used a lot of energy and didn't even realize it."

Maeve slowly sat straight, forcing KB to release the embrace, wiping her nose with the back of her hand. "Thanks for the info, Charles. I appreciate your honesty. And I apologize for the outburst. It had nothing to do with you."

"The truth is always best, I wish it were better news but now you know. Regardless, you will see them again. And soon."

"No need to apologize, Maeve," Samuel called from across the room. "We're used to drama and it was actually a wonderful demonstration. We'll all be a little more cautious around you." He placed his arm on her shoulders where KB's had been and told her simply, "Better out than in, darling. All that frustration held in can damage you more than you know."

KB and Sarah locked eyes across the room. Something was strange with Samuel. He was the same, only different. They both knew he wanted something from Maeve, yet hadn't figured out what. They didn't understand, nor would he let them intuit, that he was planning to get to Charlotte through Maeve. And if Charlotte wouldn't marry him, he was assessing his chances with this powerful new young woman. After all, Charlotte had kept him on the sidelines of her life as she took many other lovers and husbands. He might adjust his ambitions but regardless, he'd have a powerful partner and plan how to take over the council.

Charles picked a frame off the floor and rehung it on the wall as he, too, noticed the interaction. As the group slowly left the office, he took Sarah's arm. "Watch Samuel. There's something odd about him. I'm not quite sure but there's something."

Sarah nodded as Charles took her other arm and turned her to face him. For a moment she was afraid he'd try to kiss her or something weird and she pulled back. Charles laughed and told her, "Don't worry Sarah. I'm not going to make a scene. I want to tell you, Abigor has reassembled Maeve's parents. They are there on the ship."

"Why not tell the group that?"

"You think Maeve won't run to Abigor if she knows they're there? She's not as mature or selfless as you think. Let her figure it out as she helps you. Only share it with KB. Samuel already knows."

Sarah realized he was right. She didn't resist as he embraced her. She was tired. He held her for a moment longer, both of them feeling the comfort of true connection before he whispered in her ear, "I don't regret anything we had although I know it was a mistake. But I do love you. If you need anything, let me know. And watch Samuel. He too kept this information from you. Perhaps for the same reason as I did but I'm not sure. There's something going on with him."

Sarah smiled and moved away. "Yes, he has an agenda he's not sharing. But he's a powerful ally so it's good he's with us regardless. Thanks Charles. I love you, too."

As she was leaving, Charles called after her, "You should let someone in. Henry would approve, you know."

She pretended she didn't hear him. But KB did as he waited for her at the foot of the stairs. Maeve and Samuel had already tucked into the car, sharing the back seat.

KB shrugged and said to a bewildered Sarah, "He's right you know."

"Perhaps," she said. "But I'm not looking for anyone's approval."

Charles watched them leave from the landing. Sarah waved and he waved back whispering quietly, "Go with the Light," before he returned to grading papers, and they headed toward Coney Island.

Chapter 17

"I love those rides," Maeve smiled as they passed the roller coaster and the giant Ferris wheel at Coney Island amusement park. "The Ferris wheel is my favorite. My dad took me here ages ago. Seems like a lifetime ago honestly." Bruce Springsteen's Dancing in the Dark played tinnily to the line waiting to board.

"Your mother wasn't with you?" Samuel asked. wondering if she'd been with him instead, almost sorry he'd pulled her from her family for so long.

"She had something, I guess. But I liked being just with my dad. We did family things too," she defended her mother. "But my mom always needed downtime. Her words, not mine."

The topic distracted KB from his drone manuals. He knew Charlotte had been with someone else if not Samuel. He shook his head and called back over his shoulder, "It's a nice ride. But I think that walk you took down the cliffs blindfolded was much more exciting."

She remembered with terror their first meeting and how he'd blindfolded her to take her to his cave. How things had changed. "It's not all about excitement. Sometimes it's nice to relax and get a different perspective, that's all. Maybe we could ride it sometime. You'll see."

KB shrugged and went back to studying. Sarah focused on the road as it turned inland and dead ended at an old warehouse. She looked at the napkin Charles had given her to check the location. "I think we're here. This must be Vincent's place." As she parked in front a flock of seagulls flew into the air from the roof, hovered over them for a moment and then landed once again.

"A little like Hitchcock's *The Birds* in white," KB said, stretching. "I've got to pee." "I'll join you," Samuel said, once again floating out of the car and following KB, his feet just brushing the ground. They turned the corner of the building where there were hundreds of cormorants drying their wings in the dead trees of the adjacent marsh.

"Check this out," he called to Sarah and Maeve. Maeve said, "Gross. Wait for a bathroom, man." Sarah agreed, "Men can be so crude,"

"Not check us out," KB laughed, "Come see these birds. They're like dinosaurs."

The two skeptical women waited a second and then walked to the corner. Just as they got there, a middle aged, pudgy, bearded man opened the door and stepped outside. Maeve noticed him, tapped Sarah on the shoulder and called, "Hey, guys?"

"Cool right?" Vincent commented in a soft, nearly feminine voice. He had a slight accent, nearly southern, that she couldn't place as he continued, "They're amazing birds. Cormorants. You know them?"

Maeve nodded, "Yeah. I love them. You must be Vincent. I'm Maeve. This is Sarah, KB and Samuel." She liked him immediately, sensing intelligence and kindness. He was wearing a Sam Adams tee shirt and jeans that were belted under his protruding belly.

He smiled and politely waited. "Hello and yes. Charles said you'd be coming. You made good time. Why not come in?" He looked around cautiously. "It's just you four right?"

"Yes, just us," Maeve assured him.

Charles had explained how one of Vincent's carnival rides had gone wrong and several people had died. He wasn't charged since the design was perfect. It was the set up and assembly that was faulty. But Vincent never recovered from the accusations, the short time in jail while he waited to be cleared of charges and the abuse the press and community had given him. He left his job, bought this warehouse and retired to consult on safety measures for the rides. He lived reclusively in the oversized warehouse with hundreds of birds, carnival rides and his computer, slipping into an eccentricity that bordered on the absurd.

Vincent held the door and ushered them in before locking two deadbolts behind them.

KB nervously turned to ask, "Hey, we're not prisoners are we?"

"Not at all but you can't be too careful." Vincent cautioned KB wisely, "You should understand that more than most."

KB smiled, realizing he'd do the same if he lived in the middle of this marsh wasteland next to a honky-tonk village.

Samuel commented wryly, "Heck, you pretty much do the same in your cave hideout up north."

KB couldn't deny it. Vincent led them into the huge space with ceilings high enough to set up entire carnival rides inside. The guests marveled at them and Vincent explained proudly, "I test them here before they go anywhere. Still," he added meekly, "They won't put my name on it for the scandal," He obviously still found the memory troublesome. However, after a moment he regained his composure. "Regardless, these are the safest rides in the world. Follow me, please."

He led them up three flights of stairs that wound around the building toward the back where he'd turned the executive office of the commercial warehouse into his apartment. The view over the marshland behind was spectacular, as was the space below: weirdly carnival minimalist using the rides for furniture but comfortable with plenty of natural light. A second stairway at the far end of the oversized office led to the roof and hovered over a complete merry-go-round with colorful horses. The cooing of pigeons and an occasional gentle flutter of wings echoed from above.

"Please sit down," Vincent motioned to the array of horses on the ride and offered, "Want a coffee? Charles explained why you're here and yes, the birds can help."
He went to make coffee but the three hung back, unready to climb onto the ride. Only Samuel had already floated onto a horse and was patting its mane, joking, "There boy, calm down." He'd chosen a blue stallion and was obviously enjoying the farce.

"Please," Vincent encouraged and motioned again to the carnival ride, "The merry go round horses are very comfortable. Honestly, it'll make you feel like a kid," he said with a smile.

"He's got a point, guys. Come on," Samuel coaxed. "The carnival is the antidote for uptight humans. You can't help but touch your inner child once you get on."

Reluctantly indulging their host, Maeve chose a caramel colored pony with a bow in his mane. She put one foot into the stirrup and swung up to sit side saddle. KB chose a black stallion and Sarah a divinely colored pink pony. They easily mounted, enjoying the anomaly of it as Vincent continued with his back toward them saying, "But we need to protect the birds more than the drones. They're living beings."

"Of course," Sarah said, reclining on her pony's rump to release her lower back.

KB teased, "Comfy?"

She and Vincent laughed. "Yes. Very much so. It was a lot of driving."

"Make yourself at home," Vincent said, "All of you. Please. And in regard to the birds, after listening to Charles and considering what you're up against, I'm glad to help. I know the gulls can screen the drones and even protect you. Anyone who's been to the Jersey shore with a bag of Doritos knows how aggressive they can be. And trust me, with my direction, my gulls are formidable. The cormorants can most certainly plant something to monitor below." He served them coffee and then sat in the center of the merry-go-round to face them. Sipping his, he made a bitter face and said, "We need a plan and a good one. Sugar?" He dropped 2 cubes of sugar, then added two more, into his coffee before he passed around the bowl.

KB took two saying, "I love these things," as he dropped three into the cup and stirred it with the small spoon Vincent had placed on each saucer.

Vincent waited a moment to let them all enjoy the beverage before he said, "Let's take this and your drones to the roof and see what they can do."

They slid off their horses to follow Vincent up the stairs as KB grabbed the drones.

At the top of the stairway, he pushed open a double door and they walked onto the roof where hundreds of seagulls perched on the edge of the building. The gulls started clucking when they saw them. They didn't fly away. Instead, they jumped down to the floor and inched closer in a nearly menacing way. Vincent went to them and made some soothing noises to settle them down.

Maeve mumbled, "Wow," and tapped Sarah on the shoulder. A huge antenna rising from the rooftop was covered in cormorants with their wings open to dry. The scene of these near dinosaurs extending their wings was simultaneously magnificent and spooky.

Vincent smiled, "Amazing right? These birds have the most incredible oil on their feathers. It allows them to live in both worlds, underwater and above. But the wings need to dry. Watch your step," he cautioned about the bird poop that was everywhere.

Samuel merely floated over it all and looked down in disgust at the layers of guano caked on the floor. "This shit isn't great for our respiratory systems, you know," he commented, "Bird poop carries over 60 diseases and parasites that can make us all super sick. We don't need to be coughing all across the harbor in this mission."

"No we don't," Vincent agreed. "But that level of

contagion is rare and I clean regularly. But yes, don't stick your face into it." He laughed as he led them to a greenhouse type building across the roof that covered a quarter of the space. Entering, Vincent confided, "This is one of my favorite places," as he lovingly drew his fingers across the tiles and chicken wire.

The space had a high tiled ceiling. Every other tile was a smoky glass and the entire back portion was open with a roll of chicken wire off to the side. "I leave it open during the day to let the pigeons come and go," he explained. "But I close it at night so they're secure."

Small cubby hole nests lined the walls with a cooing pigeon inside each. In some, two huddled together. Maeve found the sound fantastically soothing. On one wall was a huge area fenced with chicken wire where small finches flew back and forth, their wings making another gentle sound.

"This aviary is my sanctuary." He brushed bird guano off a long table that lined the center.

"Are these homing pigeons?" Maeve asked.

"Yes. Very special birds." He touched the beak of one opalescent gray bird and she rubbed it against his palm. He finished nostalgically, "Some have brought me messages from as far south as the Caribbean and as far west as the Mississippi. They have longer battery life than those drones of yours."

"Amazing," KB said, genuinely appreciating all of it as he put the drones on the nearly clean table.

Sarah noticed that the gulls and cormorants had slowly followed them and were moving like a wave around the door. "Is it feeding time?" she asked nervously.

Vincent laughed. "They like to be near us. Perhaps for food. I think they're curious and instead of waiting for their next meal, they'd rather feed themselves. They're relatively wild. I give them love and a safe place to rest. And, yes, some snacks. We play or if you prefer to call it training, we do that. It's a special relationship. You may not understand but if you work with me for a while you will." He took the drones from their cases.

Samuel listened carefully. Too carefully, Sarah thought to herself. She was still struggling to get into his mind as KB reviewed their capabilities and the idea to monitor what was going on off New York Bay.

"The drones are a good idea," Vincent said, "But they'll stand out. Especially that far off shore. Even a bird at that distance is something to note." A pinkish gray pigeon jumped to his shoulder and he continued, "Tell me. Once you figure out what they're doing, what do you plan to do about it?" Only the cooing of the pigeons and the odd cluck of a gull filled the silence. Vincent pushed the issue asking, "How will you change it? Do you have a plan?"

Maeve spoke first, "We need to know what we're up against regardless and what they are working on, no? Now I know my parents' molecules are on that boat so, I mean, how can we make a plan without that knowledge. I can't lose them to the sea again."

Vincent exhaled. "Listen. You have very few resources and it's pretty fair to assume those ships are up to no good. The mere fact that they are there, cloaking and basically using slave labor should be enough. Do you actually need to know what they're doing below the water to stop what they are doing above? Stopping what they're doing above will take care of below. Besides, the level we can manage, your parents will stay there."

"It might also give us the time to eventually investigate below." KB said. "But the knowledge would give us an advantage since, as you say, we're outnumbered and outgunned. And help us find your parents in whatever state," Sarah noted.

Samuel nodded agreement.

"Outnumbered perhaps but outgunned?" Vincent shook his head and said, "Not necessarily. You can use your drones to monitor but you can also use them to create fear and a distraction. Particularly if we mask them with our bird friends." Vincent got excited as he spoke, "We let the gulls create a major distraction and shield a drone from above. We use the cormorants to take the second drone below to get information while we take on the ship at the surface."

"Wow," KB said. "Are you proposing to confront Abigor and the Shadows with our power and seagulls?" He smirked. "Vincent, no disrespect intended, but have you ever interacted with Shadow force? And this Captain?"

"I have. We can discuss that another time. It may help you. This Captain, Abigor, is well known here in the beach area. He's following a long line of sea-faring people who supply some of the wealthiest families in the world with whatever they need; drugs, slaves, contraband materials and animals. They've been around for ages, generations of wildcats that some called Robin Hoods of the sea and some called pirates, others criminals. My point, however, is that we don't have the resources for 2 strikes so we should make one, make it soon and make it count."

"Well," Sarah interjected, "Unlike pirates we don't need to take the ship. We only need to disable their operation, free their people and get enough intel to make it public."

"What's their weakest point?" Samuel asked. "Got to be that umbilical cord," Sarah said.

"You're talking about where the supplies come in and out?" Vincent asked. "How'd you know about that?" Sarah asked.

"Fishing communities know everything. You are not the first boat to notice something. You're just the first to understand the implications and actually do something about it."

"KB what about that TV you have where we saw them first?" Maeve asked, "Could we use that for air intel? Or at least to see where we should send the drone and the gulls?"

KB seemed annoyed that she'd mentioned his TV, especially since Samuel perked up to hear more. But KB regained composure quickly and said, "If I go back upstate and take a look, I can tell you. The thing is, there's no directing the picture. I get an overall view but can't say from where it's coming."

"So that's how you've been spying. It shows you their operation?" Samuel asked. "Yeah, it gives me glimpses into the Shadows' daily activities and it's not pretty. I used some very old technology to tap into what they've been doing.

That's why we came to find you. I've known about this for a while, apparently like the entire community here."

"Can you remember, KB, any point that seemed particularly vulnerable apart from the umbilical cord?" Vincent asked, "Let me explain why. They must know that's their most vulnerable point. It's where the drones were triggered when you got close. It's their most important place to protect. So, while hitting them there makes sense, it will be where they can strike back the fastest and hardest. We need to surprise them. Another point that's nearly as vulnerable but where they wouldn't expect would be better."

"Good point," KB said, brightening. "I know. At the helm. Where their leadership hangs out. It's also where they have charts, monitoring and control equipment. It's all windows as well. The gulls can make a huge mess there."

"They don't even need to break the windows. They can blind them with poo," Samuel commented looking at the mess on the floor in disgust. "This stuff can be fatal if inhaled, you know."

Vincent laughed. "Well, like I mentioned, you have to breathe in the dust, which we're not doing here, Samuel. But you're right. And the gulls don't get too close or hurt. The drone can fly close and shoot from above before the birds start. While they're scrambling at the helm, we'll send the cormorants down with the drone and a little plastic explosive."

"Wait a minute," Sarah said. "How 'little' on the explosive?"

"This is moving pretty fast for me," Maeve said.,

"When did we become environmental terrorists?"

"When the odds became so grand," Samuel said.

"Well," Vincent continued, "If you want to get someone's attention, you need to make a lasting first impression. This won't be over with this one attack so, if you can't win outright, you'd better get some respect at least. Think about it. Are we ok with the explosive?" he asked and then waited.

Vincent looked at their stunned faces. "Right then. We are unanimous. Photos and a disabling explosive it is," he smiled. "So KB, we've got to modify the camera so it's good underwater. Help me out here, will you?"

KB and Vincent opened the drone, and Vincent sprayed the inside with silicon, gently waterproofing the battery and internal mechanisms.

"That is one fine waterproofing," KB commented.

"I love this stuff," said Vincent. "We used to put it on the roller coaster carts for the rides where they'd go into water. Those big splashes can rust and erode things fast. It's amazingly light so it won't affect the operation of this little guy." He finished the inside, put a small piece of tape over the lens and sprayed the outside. "That should do it," he said looking satisfied.

KB asked, "Will you strap this onto the bird? Because I doubt it can move by itself underwater."

"Exactly the idea, KB," said Vincent ignoring his sarcasm. "These cormorants can descend up to 150 feet, that's about 50 meters. But I have one or two who are able to go deeper. Now even though the Atlantic Ocean has an average depth of more than 3000 meters, the area off the Hudson River and into the bay is about 65. They're dredged to that depth for commercial traffic from the Port of Albany to New York City. The Captain isn't that far off the coast and I imagine that even though he's close to the bottom, he is not at the bottom, unless it's purely robotics in that mechanism below the sea, our yellow submarine if you will."

"You think the birds can make it?"

"They won't have to," Maeve chimed in. "There are zoom lenses on these things, right? I mean they are basically flying go-pros. You could have bought one of those, too, come to think of it. KB and Vincent nodded and she continued. "So all we have to do is enable the zoom to the max and get the lucky bird to swim close enough and aim appropriately to get the shot. Have you trained them for that?"

Vincent explained, "I've trained them to retrieve things. Their comprehension of what I want is incredible but it's not like I can explain to this bird exactly what we're up to, step by step. We communicate in a way and they understand, but the details," he paused, "Well that's her call. We'll send my friend Chloé, " When he said the name, one of the cormorants came closer. "And she needs to drop the explosive as well."

"They know their names?" Samuel asked.
"I talk to them and they hear, so, yes. They know their names." Vincent replied. "You said there was some light. I'm betting that Chloé will go for the light and when she realizes it's too deep, drop the explosive and come back to the

surface."

"Betting?" KB said.

"Listen. These are birds, not machines. I can't guarantee anything. We'll all meditate with the focus to send them where we want. You understand that your thoughts have power, right? So when the birds go into action we need to be behind them 100% mentally and send them the energetic direction to dive. We are truly all connected. Are you with me on that?"

They nodded in unison.

"Good. We'll practice that in a minute because the birds like to explore in the early morning and late afternoon." He thought for a moment. "You know, we could manage this at first light. I see no reason to wait."

"Perfect, we practice with the birds, rest and get on it in the morning," Maeve said.

"Yeah, I'll feel a little more certain hanging with the birds a bit. Give them a sense of us and yes, practice visualizing," Sarah concurred.

Samuel told the group, "First light is a very powerful time."

Vincent asked, "KB? You good with this?"

"It's about the best option we have. I actually love it," he smiled. "And yeah, just before dawn."

"All right," said Vincent. "Let's put these drones in the air and see how the gulls react."

Chapter 18

Vincent took the machines off the table and the group walked outside to the middle of the rooftop, the birds following them in an ever swaying parade. When the humans stopped, the birds did so as well but continued to shift their bodies from side to side.

After a while, Vincent said, "I'll work on the how while you all try to connect with these wonderful animals." He directed, "Sit on the floor and let the birds settle in around you." He sat down as well and said softly, "Breathe and visualize connecting. You've all meditated, right? Close your eyes if it helps." They sat relatively still and did as Vincent told them. Everyone relaxed, even the birds let their eyes soften and close. After a few moments, Vincent whispered, "I'm leaving you here now to work downstairs. Stay still. Let them get to know you." As he stood slowly to go back downstairs, a few birds followed him toward the door but, once he closed it behind him, they waddled back to the four humans sitting quietly in the center of the roof.

"This is a little weird," whispered Maeve softly.

"I'm nervous," Sarah commented as a gull walked up to her and pecked at the floor in front of her.

"That's what we're working on," KB coached them. "We need to feel good around these birds and they need to feel good around us. Be still and let them get to know you." As he spoke, a gull landed next to him and rested his white and orange beak on KB's shoulder. KB slowly turned his head toward the gull, purposefully smiled, closed his eyes again and returned his head to center. Maeve and Sarah practiced similarly; as the birds came closer they smiled and closed their eyes. Samuel was the only one who'd been deep in meditation from the start. He levitated and hovered slightly off the floor. After a full 20 minutes with Mona Lisa smiles on their faces and eyes closed, the birds gently settled around them.

Eventually, Maeve shifted her legs to relieve pins and needles in her feet. The birds shifted as well. But they didn't panic. One cormorant jumped to her thigh and spread her wings gently. Maeve opened her eyes to notice the bird's exquisite turquoise eyes and the reptilian texture of the bird's orange beak. Two other cormorants moved onto Sarah's folded knees and rested there, again, wings open and facing her. "They're amazing," whispered Maeve as the two pre-historic relics nestled into Sarah's knees and relaxed.

Samuel had a cormorant resting on each shoulder and a gull was comfortably nesting in KB's lap. KB was smiling almost foolishly, finding the whole scene pleasurable and whispered, "Now's the time to see if you can connect. Feel their heartbeat and send positive, loving emotions."

As they did, the animals came even closer. A few pigeons came from the coop and wandered into the group, finding spots as close as possible. The finches stopped their frenetic activity and relaxed in their oversized cage, tucking their beaks into their wings to rest. Everything calmed down.

"Slowly, slowly, start to stand," KB commanded.

"What do I do with these birds on my lap?" Sarah

asked quietly.

"Take them with you," KB instructed, "Embrace them and lift them up."

Ever so slowly they stood, carrying the birds that had come to their laps and pushing themselves to their feet; Maeve crossed her legs and stood with a cormorant on each extended arm. KB cradled a gull and Sarah allowed two cormorants to move to her shoulders as she stood with a pigeon gently resting on the crown of her head.

Samuel finally let his feet touch the ground as he supported the two cormorants on his shoulders. The rest of the army of birds slowly moved closer, making subdued cooing and clucking sounds.

"Shuffle your way over to the antenna, ok?" KB instructed.

Sarah, Samuel and Maeve followed slowly and relatively gracefully to the antennae, with the birds like a gentle gray and white mist across the roof. At the antenna, KB said, "Now focus on having them, at least the ones closest to you, move to the antenna. Visualize it happening."

They stood still and visualized the birds taking flight. After a moment, the gull in KB's arms opened his wings, rubbed his beak softly against KB's cheek and gently floated from his arms to settle on the antenna. The cormorants who had been on Sarah's shoulders bent their knees and jumped to the antennae as gracefully. They worked into a space on the metal arms and, once again, opened their wings. Maeve mentally encouraged her avian friends to move and lifted both closer so they could hop on and join their friends. Samuel floated with the gulls to accompany them onto the steel arms. He gently let them go and returned to the ground slowly.

"Encourage them to settle in. Think loving thoughts," KB instructed.

For the next five minutes they stood and meditated. The birds gently went onto the antenna or nestled into spaces close by, some on the floor and a few in cardboard boxes that were scattered across the rooftop.

"Now visualize them all moving into flight," KB suggested.

The gulls started first. After a few seconds, they shifted and about a dozen caught the air and moved in a circle around the roof. Coming back to retrieve more, they made a wider circle as KB, Samuel, Maeve and Sarah stood, mentally petitioning them to fly. In several ever growing circles all the gulls were in the air together, playing. They moved like a wave, each one synchronizing, rising and falling with the air currents and each other. Then the cormorants shifted and flew below them, not as gracefully but with purpose. They lifted off the antenna and came back, playing with the gulls as the pigeons rose as one into the sky, banked and returned with the group.

The humans smiled as the birds created a moving masterpiece in the sky. KB whispered, "Ask them to return." Together they focused and watched as the flock came back to rest around them.

"Amazing," Maeve commented, lovingly touching a gull's head.

"Well done," Vincent applauded from the doorway as the birds slowly moved toward him in welcome. "That was exactly what I needed to see. They've connected with you now. Meditation is so powerful. So let's take this one baby in the air with them." He placed the drone on the floor and directed the group to meditate again, asking the flock to cover the drone. Vincent started the machine and the subtle hum of its motor called their attention. Distracted, they started to disperse. Vincent advised them, "You'll need to capture their attention once again. Focus."

They closed their eyes and visualized the birds soaring around the machine as it rose and banked to the left horizontally, Vincent manning the controls. The birds reluctantly moved into the air around the humming drone as the humans meditated and visualized them camouflaging it. Vincent smiled and took the black box higher. The humans followed mentally and the gulls moved with their thoughts. Samuel levitated off the floor and floated with the birds rising and falling around him. "Wonderful," Vincent whispered as he brought the drone down and the gulls gently followed.

"Well done," he said to both the gulls and his new human friends. "Let's feed them and let them rest. We'll do the same tomorrow only with a more focused plan. I've been working on something. Let me show you."

Chapter 19

The birds followed them back to the aviary with that clumsiness that characterizes grounded beings of flight. The flock gathered in the doorway as the humans moved to the table. Vincent took a large drawing and the second drone from the bag on his shoulder. It was in pieces and he placed the pieces on the table next to the other.

"It was good to take this one apart," Vincent assured KB, noting his distress before he tossed bread crumbs onto the floor on the other side of the roof. He continued to explain, "I know. It looks a mess. But now I totally understand the mechanics and I'm sure the cormorant can take this camera down. It's tiny and light and won't affect her mobility under water. I've modified a headlamp strap so she can wear it like a helmet." He held up the small camera and a tiny bathing cap complete with chin strap to the group, looking at it and saying satisfactorily, "Not bad honestly. With the support and the chin strap she won't lose it or be uncomfortable."

"Did you have a particular bird in mind?" Maeve interjected.

"Chloé, remember? But several will go down. I'll introduce you in a moment." Vincent rolled plans onto the table. The first sheet was a map of the area. "We'll leave from here." He pointed to a spot that marked a dock close to the warehouse. "Sarah, you'll have to bring your boat from the mooring. Perhaps you and KB can go for it once we're done. Tie up there at the marina. I'll speak with the owner so you have a slip."

Sarah gave him a thumbs up and was already out the door, but Vincent called her back.

"Here's the chart of the area we'll go to tomorrow," Vincent said, noticing with some discomfort that Samuel had moved closer to him. Something told him Samuel had conflicting priorities. "Let's make space for everyone," he told him and elbowed him slightly so he could float a little farther away and everyone could see the plans. "The gulls will follow in the air. The four cormorants will come with us so they're not exhausted before we arrive. It's a long way," he explained as he rolled the next plan open.

It was a cross section and Vincent had drawn several trajectories above and below the water. "The gulls will come in here, above and in front of the boat, surrounding the drone which will hover over the entire operation. If we time it early, around breakfast, they may think the birds only want food and won't get suspicious too quickly. The key is to be guiding the animals mentally. If you get distracted, they will too. That will be you, KB, and Samuel. I'll be manning the drone and Sarah will be driving the boat. Maeve, you'll guide the cormorants. Think you can do it?" he asked the group.

KB commented, "Shouldn't you work with the birds and I man the drone? I mean, they know you."

"He's got a point," Samuel added.

Vincent told him, "I'm too close. I won't let them be in danger. I'll sacrifice a drone but I'll call the birds off if it gets too risky. It's better if both of you do it. I know you can." He assured KB and Samuel by putting a hand on each shoulder to get acquiescence. "From the back, by the umbilical cord, the cormorant group will go down as deep as they can. This is the 'piece de resistance'," he said with flair. "I've got a plastic explosive they'll drop on the lab that will disable it and force it to the surface so that we can get a good idea of what they're up to. We all need to work our cloaking skills and stay outside their field of consciousness. Once the birds go down they can find their way home. We'll call Chloé back and take the camera and then let her decide. If they stay in the boat they'll have a ride. But they may prefer to swim. The gulls will stay around the ship with the drone so we can film what they're up to. They'll fly back with us."

They nodded, and Vincent summarized, "We're finished in less than 10 minutes. Remember, they have guns on that ship," he ran his fingers through his hair. "And a load of black magic." He nodded, as if telling himself it would be ok. "The gulls will recede after they've made a mess of the windshield and the bow, confusing and blinding them."

Sarah interjected, "That'll bring a few people up from below. So we can learn more about them as well."

"Exactly," said Vincent, "But it won't be much. Less than 10 minutes and we're done. We're outgunned and need to make this quick. Same thing for the birds in the water. In and out. Pray for a relatively calm day. It'll make everything easier."

The group nodded agreement as Maeve said, "I need to upgrade my cloaking skills."

KB agreed, "For sure."

"Stay here and work a bit with me and Samuel while Sarah and KB go for the boat. We'll get you up to speed," Vincent assured her.

"Right," Sarah said. "KB? Let's go, then."

"Right," KB said.

"Right," Vincent echoed.

"All right," Maeve mimicked.

Samuel laughed and confidently told them, "We got this," as Vincent rolled the plans and they started toward the door.

Maeve called to them as they walked away, "I'm going to stay up here for a while if that's ok. See you in a few."

"I'll be back to work on your cloaking," Vincent told her as he followed Sarah and KB downstairs to open the ever-bolted front door.

Maeve wandered to a corner of the building as the carnival rides in the distance geared up for the evening. For a moment, she stopped thinking of anything. Her life seemed surreal, as if she'd entered another dimension. No nine to five, no schedule, no family, no parties, no boyfriend. But she noticed how good she felt despite a certain longing for what had been her normal. Aching for the comfort of that old life, she felt a poke on her upper thigh.

A cormorant had walked over to her. She touched its head, feeling the slickness of it. As she would a puppy, she scratched its oily feathers and the bird closed her eyes as if to say, "No regrets. Be here with me." She gently caressed the oily head until she heard the meow of a cat. Startled, she turned and saw that Oliver, the gray and white cat Kitty had always shifted into, had somehow joined them and was sauntering toward her.

"What are you doing here?" Maeve asked as he pushed his head into her hand, relishing the affectionate scratches she gave him. "Seriously, Oli, what's up?"

As she said it, he backed away and spoke to her in Kitty's tinkling sweet voice saying, *"Beidh tú ceart go leor. Táimid leat."* She understood his Irish but was fixated on watching the cat speak and hearing Kitty tell her lovingly, "You'll be fine. We are with you." He purred but then, as suddenly as he'd appeared, hissed and spat at her to comment harshly in English, "But remember, they all want you. Samuel especially. Be careful of your own." The cormorant retreated and Maeve reached for the angry feline cooing, "Oliver." But he leapt from the roof. Maeve reached for him, breathless and watched as he spread his arms and legs and caught the air to fly into the horizon. He disappeared in seconds leaving Maeve to wonder if he'd been there at all.

She rubbed her eyes and searched the sky and then the ground for him as the door opened and Vincent came back with Samuel saying, "Let's get to work."

Maeve nodded, not wanting to share this latest anomaly, and only mumbled, *"Ar aghaidh linn."*

Samuel smiled and raised an eyebrow as he floated toward her and repeated her comment in English, "Yeah, let's."

Chapter 20

"Glad you're bonding. That's Chloé. She's our deep diver. I've watched her stay under for nearly 5 minutes and retrieve objects from just under 60 meters," Vincent called to her.

The cormorant had waddled back to Maeve's side and she kept her hand on the bird's head as she told him, "That's nearly 200 feet! She's our cohort tomorrow, right?"

He smiled and said, "Yes, actually, she'll carry the camera and the explosive. She loves a deep dive. It'll be Chloé, Boa and T Rex over there."

Hearing their names, the two fluttered their wings. They were the largest of the group. Compared to them, Chole was petite. "They are amazing birds. Right," Vincent inhaled the word, "Let's get to work. We've got a little more than an hour. Let's talk about cloaking, shall we?"

"Tell us what we can help you with," Samuel asked Maeve, "It seemed you had it down when you bumped into my car back there."

"Yes and no," Maeve said, "I understand the concept and all. I'm just not good. Well, sometimes I am and then sometimes not so much." She felt the heavy weight of her responsibility and somewhat of a failure at so many of these practices.

Samuel took her chin and consoled her, "No one learns this automatically. Have you ever watched a baby learn to walk? Step by step, right? You've done amazingly well to learn it at all."

"So we'll practice," Vincent told her. "Step by step.

I like that, Samuel." They sat down with Chloé standing behind them, opening her wings. "Give it a try," Vincent said.

Samuel coached her, "Close your eyes. Breathe, and visualize an amazing white light around you. Let it emanate from your belly button."

Maeve did as he said and relaxed into his guidance. She took a deep inhale as Samuel continued, "Now let that light become a mirror and reflect everything around it. The sky, the buildings, even the birds and the antenna."

Again, she focused.

"Stay with that image and breathe. Keep your eyes closed," he directed.

Little by little the mirror image of the landscape around Maeve enveloped her. She became invisible for a moment. Then the mirror fluttered and her shape returned. "Take a deep breath and relax," Vincent told her. "You had it but you lost focus. Try again."

"Don't panic. It's just like meditation," Samuel told her.

She nodded, closed her eyes once again and visualized the light around her. Her shape became translucent, a foggy mirror of the surroundings, her outline faint in the afternoon sky.

"Breathe and focus," encouraged Vincent.

She did and finally faded from sight. The birds stayed close, feeling her but no one would have seen her sitting among them. She settled in. Vincent meditated next to her. Samuel moved to the birdhouse to look over the plans once again.

"Hey Vincent," they heard the call from below. Sarah and KB had returned.

Maeve's cloaking flickered and Vincent stood and said, "I'll let them in. Keep practicing. You are doing amazingly well." He walked across the roof with a few birds following him to the door. Samuel was still reviewing the plans. "Everything still clear? Any comments?" Vincent called to him.

"Crystal," Samuel told him without looking away.

Vincent nodded, wondering at Samuel's obsession with the ship's plan but accepted it as his way of preparing for battle. He jogged down the stairway and called, "Coming," before he undid the deadbolts.

"How's it going?" Sarah asked as KB followed her in. "We left the boat at the dock, just like you said. Sweet set up there, honestly. KB and I could stay there if you prefer. It's just a few hours."

"Don't be silly," Vincent told her, refastening the deadbolts behind them. He walked them up to the roof. Pushing the door open, Sarah asked, "How'd she do?"

"Well you can see," he chuckled, "Or not."

They saw a flash like a short circuit in the corner where Maeve was sitting, cloaked. Slowly her figure came into focus. "Voila," said Vincent. "She's been cloaking for nearly the entire time you've been away." He turned to Maeve and said, "Well done!"

Samuel strolled from the bird house and told them,

"She's a natural."

A chill ran up Sarah's spine as he said it but she wasn't sure why. She had no idea that he'd reviewed the plans with the intention of finding a moment to take Maeve to her parents and win her never ending gratitude, or love. He wasn't sure which would be more beneficial to his plans.

"Amazing," KB smiled, almost proudly, "How do you feel?"

"Quite energized actually. I almost wanted to stay," she confided.

"Wonderful work, Maeve," Sarah congratulated her, shaking off a feeling of impending complications.

Maeve smiled and asked, "How'd it go with the boat?"

"Great," KB answered. "And it looks like smooth seas for tomorrow."

"Fantastic," Vincent commented. "Even more importantly, it looks like you've all bonded with the birds. Notice they didn't fly away when you arrived. Quite the contrary, actually. We had no idea when you drove in."

The quiet birds had edged closer. Once again Chloé was at Maeve's side. She gently pressed her weight against Maeve's leg as a reminder of her presence.

"When you were cloaking they were all waiting for you, Maeve. They felt you and settled in. It was lovely to watch," Samuel told her.

"Great," Sarah said, "Let's get some food then and some rest. You don't mind takeaway?"

"I'll actually go pick it up" Vincent said, "I don't love for just anyone to come here."

163

"Better," KB defended Vincent. "It's not paranoid either. More cautious and safe. I appreciate it and I'll go if you like."

"Thanks, but I could use a walk. There's a great Thai place around the corner. Come downstairs so I can show you where you'll sleep. You can all have a shower too if you like."

"Actually," KB said guiltily, "We showered at the marina. Couldn't resist."

"That means the hot water's all mine," Maeve said smiling as they walked to the stairs and said so long to the birds who congregated by the door.

"Don't forget to leave a little for me," Samuel reprimanded her good naturedly.

Chapter 21

Far from the coast in the northern forest, Mary's long grey and black hair fell around her face as she gazed into the glass top table. Kitty and Sadie stood beside her, their heads wrapped in colorful scarves as they all swayed back and forth, mumbling in Irish, *tabhair dúinn an fhírinne, tabhair dúinn an solas, tabhair dúinn an ionadh, tabhair dúinn an gchumhacht, feicfimid ár gcailín anocht!* "See the truth, see the light, see the wonder, see the might, let us see our girl tonight!"

The tabletop became a mirrored image of Maeve as she touched Chole's beak.

The three sages could see her on the rooftop at Vincent's. Kitty smiled lovingly but nervously played with a rhinestone button on her cardigan, "I told you she was great. Not sure why you need to spy on her like this." She was still unsure of her sisters' intention with their surveillance.

But Sadie called into the image, "Good, good my girl. You're still learning." She clapped her hands gleefully and told Maeve, "Yes, that's it. Befriend them all. The animals will save you. And wait 'til you see what you're up against. Then you'll see my plan was right. You'll understand it's not so easy. The Grounds fall into Shadow so easily."

Kitty and Mary continued to hold the spell, swaying and chanting. Mary's hair brushed in front of the image each time she swayed to the left and Sadie had to keep pushing it away so that she could see. "Couldn't you tie that hair back.

Or get a scarf," she scolded her sister.

Mary only laughed and continued, exclaiming, "I like it down. It feels more enchanting somehow."

Her sister snorted, "Hmfffff, it's getting in my eyes and blocking my view."

Kitty touched the scarf on her head and said, "We each move to our own rhythm, Sadie. If the council hadn't shaved your head, you might be doing the same."

"Head shaved, powers stripped," Mary interjected and then added, "You might practice a little gratitude that your sisters still hold their power and are willing to help." The picture flickered as Mary and Kitty were distracted and Sadie said, "Oh all right. Thank you. Please, keep the vision going. We need to see what they're up to. She defied me and we both could have died in that fight. But she's still my protégé. Now more than ever, honestly. If the council sends me into the ether early, there'll be no one left. We need to make sure she understands her role."

"You mean **you** need to, Sadie. I see her as working out quite nicely. She's met all the right people," Mary commented.

"She is managing nicely," Kitty agreed. "Her skin looks polished. You'd never guess how badly it was damaged," she added, referring to the boils and pustules that had covered her entire body after her battle with Sadie. She leaned closer to the table and put her hand on the image of Maeve's face and purred, "Perfectly healed."

"But she needs to see the bigger picture. The bigger threat to the planet, our dear mother earth. It's not just these mad projects the Shadows are pushing. It's the support they get from the Grounds. Look," Sadie admonished her sisters, "None of these projects would be imaginable if it weren't for Grounds' consumer frenzy and their inability to support each other."

"She'll see it when she starts to fight them. Don't be such a control freak, Sade," Mary chastised. "Let things take their course. After all, you'll be seeing the council next week."

"Perhaps you should be working on your defense," Kitty recommended and walked away from the table as the image flickered out of focus.

"Kitty's right, you know. We have more important things to do than to practice this voyeurism, pretending to be able to help." Mary stood to stretch as the gray and white cat Oliver wrapped itself around her ankles, petitioning for attention. She walked to the edge of the patio and the image disappeared. "You've seen she's ok. Let's get back to how you'll defend your future to the council next week."

Chapter 22

Descending into the warehouse, Vincent showed them to a corner space where a carnival ride lay open in organized pieces on the floor.

"This is a circular ride that I unraveled. It was for 4 people sitting facing each other so I pretty much peeled it open and turned the chairs into guest beds. Don't worry, I created a softer and more supportive cushion. It's memory foam."

"Got to love repurposing," Sarah commented smiling.

He continued, "There are linens in the bath over there. The hot water takes time, but I collect it in the bucket as I'm waiting and use the excess to flush the toilet or water the plants. I hate to waste water. It's so precious, you know?" he called to them over his shoulder as he walked away. They heard him lock the 3 deadbolts behind him as he left to get takeaway.

"I feel safe," KB commented, raising an eyebrow and bouncing up and down gently on one of the beds before laying back and admitting, "These beds are amazing."

Samuel was hovering skeptically over his, until KB's comment and he slowly lowered himself onto the makeshift bed. "You're right," he agreed.

Sarah brought the linens and started to make the beds while Maeve showered. "I'm going up to the roof for a moment, ok? Seems you've got bed making sorted," KB teased with a smile.

Sarah laughed good heartedly. She knew men who assumed you'd take care of them and explained to KB, "Actually, why not you and Samuel make the beds. I'll do the pillow cases. Get on either side of these beds before you go."

"Happy to help," Samuel said.

KB mumbled agreement, confused that it was an issue. After all, he could make them all in a flash. So could Sarah. He'd never loved teamwork but he acquiesced. Once they tucked in the last corner, he winked, "Voila," before he left them and climbed the stairs to the roof to watch the carnival lights that dotted the evening sky, unsuccessfully competing with the stars. He could faintly hear the carnival music. The birds congregated around him, some even touching him with their heads.

He whispered, "Listen guys. Tomorrow's a big day. We have to take care of each other. These other people are powerful." He took a breath before continuing, "They believe in themselves like we believe in us. Honestly, they may think they are doing the right thing. That's what's so weird." He mused and then mumbled, "What the….." as he saw Vincent walking back with takeaway and two men pushing him along on the street below. One was pushing something into his waist. KB realized it was a gun. He watched them come to the door of the building before he pushed off the railing and ran downstairs, calling "Guys! Come up here. Fast."

The birds around him, sensing his nervousness, clucked and flapped their wings. Sarah and Maeve walked toward the stairway with inquisitive looks on their faces as the keys turned noisily in the deadbolt and they heard male voices impatiently mumble behind the door, "Can't you move faster?" and the shuffle of feet before a thud and a groan.

"Upstairs, quickly," KB ordered the two women as Samuel nearly flew to the top of the stairway. KB opened the door for them and instructed, "Stay with the pigeons. Cloak."

Maeve and Sarah nodded and closed the door quietly as KB descended to wait behind the entry. Samuel came downstairs as well, winking toward the now cloaked KB, "I've got your back," as he too sparkled into nothingness and they both disappeared from sight. The last deadbolt released and Vincent was pushed into the room. He stumbled to keep his balance but the bag of food fell to the floor, duck sauce and spring rolls rolled across the concrete.

Kevin and Mark, the two thugs who'd pushed Maeve into the PCB muck in the first place then pursued her to near destruction as she fought her ancient aunt and who'd just missed catching them at Sarah's house, now followed Vincent inside. They mumbled, "Crazy shit," as they took in the immensity of the area surrounding them. Vincent pulled his shirt back down to meet his pants and touched a stain on it before moving the hand to his lip and realized he was bleeding. KB hid behind the still open door, invisible.

"Where's the rest of your gang?" Mark asked Vincent. "I know you weren't going to eat all that Thai yourself."

Vincent didn't answer but straightened his spine and

stood tall as the two thugs walked around. Kevin sat on one of the horses in the merry go round. Mark looked inquisitively at the rides, noticed the beds on the floor and said, "You planning a pajama party?"

At that moment, KB slammed the door and ran an invisible leg under Mark's feet to knock him over. Kevin pointed the gun in Mark's direction but wasn't sure where to fire. He stumbled off the horse he'd been sitting on and nervously shot into the space around him. The bullet ricocheted off a steel beam before it embedded itself into the wall by the door. "Damn it Kevin, don't shoot until you can see what you're shooting at," Mark yelled as KB hit him in the stomach and he doubled over, groaning.

Vincent grabbed an oversized wrench and ran behind Kevin to hit him in the head. As the tool fell onto his skull, Kevin turned and grabbed Vincent's wrist to pull him into a headlock. He pushed the gun into Vincent's temple and called in a voice filled with desperation and pain as blood wandered down his forehead, "Show yourself or I'll blow his head off. And don't doubt that I will."

A flash of light illuminated the corner behind the doubled over Mark as KB became visible. With a satisfied grin on his face, he threatened Kevin, "I don't doubt you'd do anything to protect yourselves. But it's too late for that." Kevin pushed the gun deeper against Vincent's skull and KB continued smugly, "You should be running from here. But it's too late for that too."

As he finished the sentence, Samuel opened the door at the top of the stairs and escorted a gray cloud down the stairs from above. Hundreds of pigeons swooped into the space to defend their master and his protector. Before Kevin could raise the gun, they had swarmed over him, pecking at his body. He dropped the gun and Vincent ran free while his attacker raised his arms to protect himself, covering his eyes with one arm and unsuccessfully trying to beat the swarm of birds off with the other. The already beaten Mark cowered in a corner with his arms overhead before crawling to hide under a table as the avian beating continued and the gray mass filled the huge space.

In a blur, Maeve sped down the stairs with a coil of rope in her hands. She pulled Kevin's hands behind his back as the birds attacked the front of his body. He screamed and pulled his bludgeoned face toward his chest to hide as Vincent vindictively kicked him in the groin. Surprised by his uncharacteristic violence Maeve asked, "You OK?" genuinely concerned by his reciprocity as she tied the now doubled over and listless Kevin tightly to the merry go round. Vincent nodded yes, puffed his chest out a bit and helped her pull a sobbing Mark from under the table by the back of his shirt to tie him as well. Tightening the knots around their wrists and ankles, Vincent gently called to his winged minions, "It's ok, my darlings," as they gradually receded and congregated around Vincent cooing. Sarah came down the stairs saying, "I'd say we bonded alright. These birds are amazing. The gulls were waiting to join but it didn't look like the pigeons needed any help."

"We should have let them finish these two off. What do we do with them now?" KB asked as he walked to the gun on the floor and picked it up. "All this for a few dollars? What's your beef with my friend Maeve?" he asked Mark and shook the gun in his face.

Mark was quiet but Kevin sobbed like a baby. Both their faces were swollen and dripping blood. Their shirts were torn and even their pants had been ripped. Blood oozed from the tears in their clothing. Mark lifted his head to speak. "It was never about the money," he said through a spittle of blood coagulating at the corner of his mouth. He spat and explained, "Digging into the entire production was only the beginning," he said to KB and continued, "There's the bigger picture. She needs to pay for her ancestors' crimes. Nothing personal, really," he spat to Maeve and then turned to KB, "You know, she's an aberration. The Shadows will eventually eliminate her, with or without us. Eventually your Light council may even want her gone."

Maeve wanted to kick him but refrained. Instead she asked, "What are you talking about? I was following a paper trail that anyone will find eventually. Your ridiculous attempt to kill me actually gave me all these powers. Ha. And I'm working for the Light. They won't ever want me gone." Exasperated, she asked the group, "Well, should we call the police or what?"

"Let's leave them here. We can deal with them later," Vincent said, stroking the head of the pigeon in his arms as he continued, "They're not going anywhere and we have work to do."

Kevin stopped slobbering and sniffed bloody snot back into his nose as he inhaled and spat a mix of blood and boogers to the floor, saying, "We have people in high places. They'll find us and you. You can't hide."

Vincent looked to KB and said, "Perhaps the van is a better place for them. But really, what should we do with them? Drop them at the police station?"

Maeve answered saying, "If we want to move out before first light, we don't have time. What if we leave them at the edge of the marsh? Tomorrow the police or someone will find them."

"And they'll twist things so we're the devils. No. We need to get rid of them," Samuel said matter-of factly.

"Are you talking about killing them?" Maeve asked, incredulously.

KB added, "They would have killed us. You realize that. And the birds. And probably torched this place afterwards."

"We can leave them upstairs with some avian guardians and take them to the police once we're finished and successful," Vincent commented as he began herding the pigeons to the roof. "There's no need to become like them. It defeats everything we're about."

Maeve nodded and walked over to their prisoners to untie them from the merry-go-round. Once they were free of the machine, she tied their hands to their feet and ordered KB, "Help me carry them up, will you?"

She took the now hog-tied Mark over her shoulder and KB dragged Kevin over the stairs mercilessly to the roof where they left them under the table in the pigeon coop. KB went to kick them but Maeve put her hand on his shoulder and held him back saying, "That's enough." He shrugged her hand off angrily and went downstairs again.

"I've salvaged most of the Thai food," Vincent called to the group as Maeve slowly followed KB down the stairs. Samuel and Sarah laughed as he put plates onto the table and helped himself to a hefty portion of Pad Thai. "Drama certainly increases your appetite," he said to no one in particular, touching his still bleeding lip. Sarah brought him some gauze with alcohol touching the cut. "This should help." We don't need any infections, that's for sure."

KB wandered to the table and helped himself to food as well. "Those two upstairs are the infection," he said as he joined Vincent.

Together the group reviewed the details of the next day between bites and before going to bed. Each one fell asleep quickly and soundly, as Vincent's memory foam magically took all cares and thoughts of the two criminals tied on the rooftop away. The night was quiet. Even the cooing of the pigeons stopped as they all escaped into sleep, dreaming of their big day tomorrow.

Chapter 23

The smell of fresh coffee wafted over the circle of carnival beds. The four became conscious but no one moved. The sound of pigeons cooing gently and the gulls clucks floated toward the ground slowly on still air. The criminals tied on the roof moaned slightly, shifting their weight from one bruised spot to the other. Everyone hung onto the moment of slumber before the day began.

Maeve stretched, said, "I'll go first" and stumbled into the bathroom. She came back and coaxed the others out of bed saying, "Let's call our power, ay?"

She sat on the side of the bed and told Samuel, Sarah and KB to do the same. They reluctantly threw back their covers and put bare feet on the cold ground, awakening from the toes first. Maeve said, "Ready?" and raised her arms over head with fingers spread wide.

"What are you doing?" KB asked.

"This will clear our energy. Takes 2 minutes." She instructed, "Reach your arms over head, fingers open and take a deep breath. We'll do 30 exhales and inhales through the nose and as you exhale pull your hands to your shoulders visualizing grabbing energy from the universe. On the inhales reach up for more. It's quick. Like this."

She demonstrated once or twice and they followed, each of them pulling energy from the sky and into their bodies through the breath. Between each round, Maeve led them in gentle twists and head circles and exactly 3 minutes later they were finished.

"Now say thank you for the new day and our success," she told them.

"Feel it genuinely," Samuel said.

"Yeah, thanks," KB chuckled.

"Seriously," Sarah said, "Thank you for this opportunity. I feel better."

They walked over to a drowsy Vincent who offered, "Coffee?" As he poured, he instructed, "We have about 15 minutes. My van's out back. We'll take the cormorants with us and the gulls will follow in flight, as we planned. Everyone remember?"

They nodded as KB took his gear out back to load the van with their equipment.

When he came back, Vincent said, "Before we go, let's all go upstairs. We'll check on our guests and meditate with the birds for a moment. A sort of team circle."

As they pushed open the door to the roof, the sleeping birds woke. The humans walked to the center and sat as the birds slowly stretched a wing and a leg, moving from one side to the other, some opening both wings at once, a few jumping into a wake up stretch before waddling toward them. Their would-be killers groaned and tried to shift their weight to either side unsuccessfully. "It's inhuman to keep us tied like this," Kevin called as they walked across the roof.

"Ignore the guys under the table," Vincent instructed as they moved to the center of the space. He continued, "They don't matter. Close your eyes and review our plans in your head, step by step. I'll outline them verbally while you visualize them."

They closed their eyes and Vincent whispered slowly, "We'll go with the cormorants downstairs to the van. When the gulls see us leave they'll follow in flight as we drive to the marina. Ever so quietly, we'll unload and walk to Sarah's boat. The gulls will stay close until we leave the dock. Then they'll continue in a cloud formation nearly over us. The cormorants will be in the boat with us."

He let their visualization take hold before he continued, his voice barely audible, "Once we get close to the ships, we'll send one drone up with the gulls. They'll keep a circle around it and keep it invisible since I painted it white. I'll operate the drone and the gulls will follow its course." Again he let everyone focus on seeing that happen before he started to whisper again, "I'll place the second camera on Chloé with her wonderful cap and she'll swim down to the lab and get photos. She'll have the explosive on her foot. She'll be curious until the depth forces her to surface. At that moment, she'll release the explosive with her beak, dropping it onto the lab. Once it touches the metal surface she'll have 10 seconds to surface before it detonates."

They all visualized the explosion.

"Chloé will make it to the surface before the explosion. When she surfaces, we'll instruct the gulls to dive bomb the ship, swooping down, making a scandal, screeching and pooing on everything." They each smiled in their reverie, imagining the ship disabled. "The explosion may break their cloaking so we can see them more clearly. But the drone, hovering above, will photograph not only the operation but the slave labor that comes to the upper deck and the submarine once it surfaces."

KB visualized seeing Marissa and his son and coming to the deck. Maeve saw her parents running toward her. And Samuel saw Charlotte pushing Vincent overboard to run into his arms. Only Sarah thought of Abigor and visualized him melting in horror that they'd taken his vessel.

In deep meditation, Vincent continued, "Once we have the photos and Chloé back in the boat, cloaking ourselves, we'll head back to shore."

The group assimilated everything.

"We'll get back safely having temporarily disabled their lab and with valuable intel into their plans. Everyone take a deep breath"

Even the birds seemed to inhale at his command and he instructed, "Exhale with the mouth, open your eyes and," he said enthusiastically, "let's go."

One by one, the seagulls circled into the air and the cormorants hopped to the wall and descended in circles mimicking the gulls in a poetic interplay of white rising and darkness descending. Maeve watched the theatrics before she closed the door and followed the humans downstairs. Kevin called to them, "Hey. You can't leave us here like this. Help us before you go."

"We'll be back before you know it," she called back to him as she descended the stairway. Even the pigeons who'd guarded the prisoners all night, finally sensed their uselessness and wandered to the edge of the building once the gulls and cormorants were in flight. As a group, they too rose and banked into the sky as if to say good luck before heading back to guard their captives. Morning was still far away yet they painted a composition of black, white and gray against the dark sky.

At the van, the cormorants were waiting. Vincent opened the back door and helped them in. Maeve and Sarah sat on the floor with the birds, Chloé at Maeve's side. Samuel sat in a lotus posture but hovered ever so slightly over the floor.

"More shock absorbing to float above," he smiled to Maeve. "You should try it," he told her.

She laughed and said, "I'm fine," as Vincent tried unsuccessfully to start the van.

After two attempts, it started, the group sighed in relief and they pulled slowly into the street, driving to the marina with the gulls circling overhead.

"Hope we don't have to make a quick getaway when this is over," Maeve joked to Sarah.

"I heard that," Vincent called good-naturedly from the front, "Trust that we'll be fine, or we won't be."

He smiled into the rear-view mirror as the headlights illuminated the dark, empty boulevard in front of them. Once at the marina, the tribe moved to Sarah's boat, clumsily yet quietly walking along the dock. At one point, a cormorant tripped on one of the un-leveled planks and squawked. Triggered by the noise, a light came on in an adjacent sailboat and the passenger came onto the deck.

Everyone stopped in their tracks.

Sarah whispered, "Cloak," and they became invisible.

The sailor saw nothing, scratched his head and went to the bow to pee. As he did so they started moving again. Several of the cormorants glided directly into the water. But Chloé, Boa and T Rex, connected energetically, knew to get in the boat. KB loaded the drones with Vincent and Maeve before he undid the lines and cast off, gently pushing the boat from the dock as Sarah started the engine and they quietly moved into the dawn.

The boat sliced through the water with the engine gently humming and running lights reflecting on the calm sea.

"Thank goodness it's calm," Sarah said quietly.

"Yes," said Vincent, "It's a good omen. Dim those running lights, will you?"

Sarah hesitated, as any captain would. She knew they weren't the only boat out before the sun. Vincent noticed her hesitation and quietly advised, "Trust that you'll feel another boat coming. You'll have time to maneuver out of their way. Pay attention and we'll be fine."

She finally obeyed and to an undiscerning eye, they were merely a disturbance in an otherwise calm sea; quietly respecting the telepathic language they shared as they created an undulating ripple that spread across the harbor. The gulls flew overhead and every so often would swoop closer to check in. The cormorants had settled confidently into one corner of the cockpit with Maeve with those who chose to swim following sporadically above and below the surface.

Finally, Sarah whispered, "we're here" and shifted the engine into neutral. Just ahead they could all see the blurriness that indicated the curtain of cloaking the Shadows had put around their vessels. Behind it you could faintly see the outline of the mother ship,

"They're careless in the early morning," KB said, "We're lucky. They must all be asleep and relaxed. Very few are focused."

"Exactly," said Vincent, "But we're wide awake. We good to go?" He asked the group in a whisper.

Even the cormorants nodded agreement. Maeve pulled on a wet suit and Vincent looked at her questioningly.

"What's that about?" he asked.

"I'm ready to go down if I need to. But I nearly froze last time," she told him and then, "Help me zip the back, will you?"

"That won't be necessary," he told her.

But Samuel pulled the zipper closed anyway.

Vincent frowned. "The birds will be fine. Chloé's prepared."

Maeve countered, "Listen, Vincent, in case you hadn't noticed, I've fallen in love with your birds and I can swim as well as they can, maybe better. If anything goes wrong, I'm going down to help. Not up for discussion. Just this time, I don't want to freeze." She finished with a smile and patted his arm.

Samuel shrugged and smiled at his friend. He wanted Maeve to go in. In fact he hoped she would and have a little trouble, not much, but enough so she'd scream and call

Charlotte to her. A mother, even one relatively detached like Charlotte, would never resist the screams of her child in distress. That way, Victor would separate from her and be an easier mark. Alone he was no match for Samuel.

The gulls circled overhead. Several came to rest on the boat. After a few moments they went up and let others rest, beautifully choreographing their breaks. Vincent and KB looked at the sky, noticing the gentle light of dawn cresting the horizon.

KB said, "It's time," and settled into a meditating posture.

Sarah left the boat in neutral and crossed her legs to meditate with KB. Maeve and Vincent helped the cormorants into the water. Samuel stood in the stern, focused and calm.

Maeve adjusted Cloe's cap and foot strap and whispered, "I'm here if you need me," as the bird floated for a second and then dove below the waves.

The humans began cloaking and Sarah's Zephyr disappeared from view. The seagulls entered into the circle of the Shadows and Vincent guided the drone into the air with the gulls. It was nearly invisible against the still dark sky, camouflaged by the massive white gulls.

"We need to move quickly," KB said softly to the group. "They'll all be awake and strong soon. Guide your team." Sarah stayed still, cloaking. Maeve shifted her seat and mentally focused on her cormorants, visualizing them gliding to the bottom and finding the sub.

A couple of gulls dove at two skinny workers who

had come up from the hold, stretching and yawning. They took no notice of what was happening above, raised their arms to send the birds away and walked toward the bow. It was the cook and his assistant, stumbling from sleep to make breakfast in the galley. Once they entered, it was quiet on the deck for a while longer. The gulls circled overhead.

Below, the cormorants continued their descent. Connected intuitively, Maeve saw Chloé nearly at the bottom, her webbed feet kicking as she moved toward the not-so-distant submarine, curiously passing the crate attached by a line to the sub. The octopus was still captive, now pale and quiet. It finally understood its predicament.

Chloé's camera filmed as she hovered above the sub and swam around it before she gently pecked the clip on her foot to release the explosive over the center of the submarine. She and her allies turned to rapidly swim back.

As the cormorants headed toward the surface, a school of minnows passed. The three chased them and in passing, pecked the octopus's crate forcefully with their beaks. The plexiglass shattered and the 8-legged creature slowly came back to life before he scurried to the depths as the cormorants surfaced, swallowed their catch and the explosion detonated. The water on the surface rippled gently from the blast.

In seconds, the crew came running to the deck. The captain ran from his quarters toward the helm. Doing so, he looked up. Gulls swooped down to bomb them with shit.

Vincent lowered the drone to the stern as people ran to the bow. From there he could see tanks of captive fish and hundreds of emaciated and scantily clad workers. All wore a large octopus tattoo on their shoulder. Vincent moved the drone closer and saw it wasn't a tattoo, it was a brand.

"They branded them?" he mumbled incredulously and took the drone lower nearly into the hold. It hovered there a second or two as his jaw dropped in fascination at the prison-like bunk beds and people wandering back and forth in the confined space. Suddenly, a face came into the screen and blocked the view. The captain reached for the drone but Vincent quickly moved it higher. Abigor cursed as KB mentally sent gulls down on him.

"Time to leave," Vincent commanded and began maneuvering the drone back toward the boat. "I've got intel and it's not pretty."

KB called the birds home while Sarah continued cloaking their ship. Maeve saw the cormorants in the distance.

They swam to the boat and all but Chloé dived under it to swim away, as if to say, "See you later. We'll swim back." Maeve scooped Chloé into the cockpit to take the camera from her head and the strap from around her ankle.

"You were so great," Maeve told her. As she did, Chloé moved her prehistoric head against Maeve's thigh affectionately before she jumped into the ocean to swim back, happy in the water and free from her uniform.

As the cormorants swam away and the gulls receded, the submarine breached the surface, smoke rising from the metal. Vincent positioned the retreating drone to hover over

185

it before the machine returned. It was a small and relatively basic research sub outfitted with several arms for taking samples. But what interested Vincent most was that it appeared to be unmanned and totally controlled from above. As it surfaced, the captain ran over and helped put huge straps underneath its hull so that they could pull it from the water.

At that moment, Vincent saw the tube and excavating devices on the bottom, hanging from the stern. "So that's it," he said to himself, "They're exploring the bottom. What are they looking for?" Sarah stopped meditating and started the engine saying, "Let's go," with an urgency that belied her outer calm. Samuel stayed calmly in the stern, searching for signs of Charlotte and Victor. Disappointed that they'd leave so fast.

KB continued cloaking as the gulls circled higher above the ship and joined the retreat. Sarah pushed the throttle forward and they headed back toward the harbor. The gulls followed her lead. Suddenly the boat jerked to a stop as something pulled them back.

"Did you feel that?" she asked Vincent who was reviewing footage with KB.

Maeve answered for him, "I did. And if you notice, we've stopped moving forward."

KB commented, "They've attached. Without seeing us, they felt us and attached a link. We have to break it."

Samuel mused, "They'd never let us get away so easily." He was satisfied he'd have another chance to find Charlotte.

"Yes. But how?" Sarah asked and added more horsepower. But they only inched slightly forward before stopping once again.

"It has to be cut at the source," Vincent said dryly. "Someone has to go back."

"I'll go," Maeve offered. "Send the gulls with me as a distraction, will you? And quickly," she said nervously, "tell me what I do."

KB instructed, "Distract whoever is attaching. My bet, it's the first mate. The captain wouldn't have the time. Get to that person, or those people, and pull their minds off us."

"Cloak well," Sarah said. "We'll help from here."

"Invisible, you could scream to distract him," Samuel said, disappointed that Charlotte had still not appeared. "And you may get a glimpse of your parents," he added.

Sarah countered, "Maeve, we'll get to your parents later, remember? Let's stick with our plan. I'd keep it quiet if I were you. But," and she turned to Samuel to say it, "follow your intuition. You'll know best in the situation."

"OK," Maeve said nervously and then, "Ask the gulls to cover me, will you?"

"No worries," Vincent said, "Listen. You'll need to get on board. The easiest way is the stern but this attachment is most likely coming from the bow. You'll need to go along the entire ship to find it. Take this from Chloé," he handed her the camera they had attached to the cormorant and an adhesive so she could fix it to her forehead, at the third eye. "At least we'll know what you're up to. We'll see what you see from here. At least for a little while longer."

She took a second, nodding hesitantly before she

exhaled, "Got it. See you soon."

With a determined smile on her face, she turned to jump into the ocean. Before she could, KB took her shoulders and pulled her close to him. "You can do this," he whispered in her ear. She felt the warmth of his body and a surge of confidence as she took refuge in him for a moment. Then, she pulled away and confidently grinned, "I know," before she dove into the cold Atlantic.

Frigid water seeped into her wet suit as she swam toward the ship undulating like a dolphin, ambivalent to the shock as adrenaline rushed through her veins. She kicked to nearly fly in at the low stern, sliding in on her belly. Once she slid to a stop, she closed her eyes and focused to cloak. Confident that she was invisible, she moved toward the bow past the emaciated deck hands who were slowly cleaning the mess the gulls had left. She passed the submarine on the starboard side where several people were checking damage.

"Good work Chloé," Maeve thought.

Abigor was involved but so preoccupied with damage control he didn't notice Maeve as she continued toward the helm. When she arrived, she looked into the poo stained window and saw three uniformed men sitting on the floor, concentrating.

"Attaching," Maeve thought as she pushed the doors open, entered and knocked some papers off a table to distract them. One opened his eyes and saw the mess, but couldn't see the cloaked Maeve. The other two stayed in meditation to keep their hold on the Zephyr while he swept the room with his hands, walking slowly, knowing someone was there. Maeve ducked under the table as he continued moving ever so methodically to find her.

"What to do?" she asked herself. She was suddenly afraid and the fear inhibited her creative mind. But she told herself, "It's ok. You can do this," and breathed deeply. As if a curtain had lifted, her inner voice suggested, "Push the table over onto them. Then run."

She pushed her back against the table she was hiding under, lifted it and used its legs to swing it toward the men. Groaning from the effort, she let the legs go and hit the guy sweeping to send him flying toward the others, the table landed on top of the three and broke the attachment. Below deck, the reconstructed Charlotte turned her head abruptly. "Maeve?" she asked no one in particular as she heard the cry from above. She stood and moved toward the bridge to see for herself.

"Mission accomplished," Maeve said, satisfied, and then ran to the bow to jump in and escape home. She was in mid-air when a hand grabbed her ankle and stopped her forward motion. She plummeted toward the ground. Her face hit the deck before Captain Abigor held her up like a large show fish.

"Finally, you've come to me," he cooed, "But not the way I wanted. And what is this?" his tone switched from fascination to anger as he pulled the small camera off her forehead. Maeve put her hand to her head where he'd ripped the adhesive and struggled, kicking a little. But she was nearly unconscious from the blow to her head. The captain smiled as she wrestled weakly against his grip and said, "She'll work.

See how she likes that. Perhaps it will convince her to work with me on a higher level, " and he let her go. She fell with a thud to the floor, hit her head again and lost consciousness.

Abigor stood over her and said, "It could have been so different, my sister. Look at the mess you've made. But you can't stop me." Then he turned and ordered, "Bring her below and clean up this mess," to the men pushing the table off themselves and picking themselves up. He stared into the tiny camera and asked it, "What are you looking for?" as the men lifted her brusquely by her hands and ankles and carried her out.

Charlotte was coming up from the hold as they carried her daughter down. She stopped them and gently touched Maeve's face saying "Mo stōr." nearly crying she repeated in English, "My darling, I tried so hard to keep you from all this. You'll grow up quickly here. But it's your destiny, I suppose. I can't fight it." She kissed her on the forehead and then watched as they carried her below before she went to speak with her son, Abigor.

Meanwhile, Vincent called, "Noooo," to the others as the Zypher surged forward. Unaware of what had happened to Maeve, Sarah smiled as she felt the boat's forward motion. She and KB stood at the helm with the wind in their faces as they raced toward shore, confident Maeve had released the hold and would catch up with them soon. But they turned abruptly to Vincent who stared into the small camera screen saying, "no, no, no," with Samuel over his shoulder as they monitored Maeve's progress.

Finally able to pull himself together, Vincent called

to them, "We've got a problem," and turned the small camera screen so they could see Abigor's contorted face searching into the lens before the image faded into blackness. He had put it in his pocket. Sarah's jaw dropped. Her momentary bliss at having been released quickly faded. She'd calculated that after all that time resisting, they had just about enough gas to get home. She wanted to scream as she backed off the throttle and they bobbed up and down on the rolling waves.

Vincent begged her, "We'll figure this out. Keep moving forward. We can't go back for her."

Sarah's admonished, "What do you mean? We can't leave her there."

KB had paled and stuttered, "I should have gone. She's too green."

"Don't add guilt to this," Samuel scolded. "It's no time for a pity party. And you don't have the power. We'll figure it out. But Sarah, keep moving forward while we gain a minute or two to think."

"We need to go in and rescue her," KB demanded.

"Of course we do. But what we don't need is to all be shackled below deck. That's no help so give me a second to think," Vincent nearly yelled.

Samuel added calmly, subtly assessing the odds on who would escape first, Maeve or Charlotte, "Let's all try thinking, not merely reacting. We'll get a solution more quickly that way."

Chapter 24

Metal brushed her face as Maeve touched her aching head and opened her eyes to see a chain dangling from her wrist. She was in shackles and seated on the floor against a wall. She tried to stand, but the chain was too short to allow it. Too, her legs were weak and her vision blurry. Through the haze she saw all these people, mostly women but some young men, moving around in the area. They seemed gray and flat, dusty and sweaty at the same time.

She called to them, her voice hoarse and her throat dry, "Hey. Hey. Help me. Hey, can you help me?"

But they ignored her and continued their tasks, like zombies, intent on relatively minor, mundane work. Some were sweeping, some polishing, some picking lice from cellmates' hair. Others were doing heavy lifting. There was little natural light but some sun and the sea breeze occasionally filtered through the few round portholes that were open. She could see the dust floating in the scarce sunlit air and she sweltered in the neoprene she'd worn for the frosty Atlantic. She'd never anticipated being caught below decks. The moment a breeze crossed her face, she breathed in the cool and noticed a door at the far end of the area. A light shone from under it.

She rattled her shackles as she lifted a hand to touch her sore head. When the breeze stopped, the hold immediately became stuffy and the air stank of fish, urine and sweat. She felt she was melting and as she touched her forehead and felt a growing moist bump there. Suspecting blood, she was relieved to see it was only sweat and she forced herself to inhale and exhale deeply despite the stench. "I'll wait for olfactory fatigue to set in," she joked with herself referring to the safety standards she'd learned for gas leaks that reminded people how after awhile, your nose won't recognize a smell as not so nice. She prayed it would kick in since she felt nauseous and didn't want to vomit on herself.

"I need oxygen to think," she said to no one in particular as she painfully expanded her lungs and diaphragm with the deep breaths. She was confused and her entire body hurt. "Don't forget who you are, Maeve," she reminded herself and remembered that she could easily pull away from the wall. But her intuition told her, "Wait. See a little more before you leave." The door at the end of the room creaked open. The fluorescent light from inside nearly blinded her as she squinted to see a man in a white coat who called, "I need four in here."

The voice was vaguely familiar and she wondered where she knew it from as four of the men who'd been lifting heavy objects went directly to him. After a few moments, they exited, each on a corner of a water-filled aquarium that carried a large octopus. He barely fit and was gray, not colorful like the one that had escaped into the ocean. His energy was dim. "I can't take this any longer," Maeve said as she pulled on her chains and easily ripped them from the wall, having seen enough.

No one reacted. They all stayed in their trance and the men continued to move the tank forward. She ran to them, took the tank in her arms and pushed the men out of the way before she entered the room to confront the man in the white coat. She dropped the tank on his foot and grabbed him by the neck as water splashed around them. Chains dangling from her wrists, she pushed him against the wall and demanded, "What is going on here?" Just as suddenly, she released her grip and shakily asked, "Dad?"

He laughed diabolically and freed his foot from under the tank as he opened his arms to embrace her. "My girl, Maeve. Amazing. Come on, all is forgiven," he coaxed her to come and hug him but something held her back. She looked around into the laboratory where several beds held patients attached by cables to the wall. They all wore headphones.

"What's going on here, Dad? You've reconstructed, I see," she quickly added, "And I love it. I'm happy to see you. You see, I've been searching for you," she explained, still confused over her inability to rush into his arms. "Searching for you and Mom. Where is she?"

"She's here Maeve," he told her and then, keeping his arms open, waiting for his embrace, continued, "Did you think I'd reassemble without her?" He paused and she moved slightly closer to him, still hesitant. "What's wrong?"

"Seems strange is all, Dad, you being here, lab coat and everything," she confided in him. "I mean, are you working on this ship?"

"Abigor saved me, Maeve. I'm not holding a grudge but it's more than I can say for you."

Maeve hesitated, wanting to cry. "It's not what you

think. I never imagined you would be drawn into that abyss. But you would have sent me. So," she hesitated before she finished, "Seems like we're even."

"I'm not keeping score Maeve, just telling it like it is. And if we are being 100% honest, Abigor has been like a son to me these last days since you let your mother pull me into that void." A silence filled the space between them and he let his arms drop to his side, a slow anger growing. Maeve wanted to hug him but something still held her back. There was something different about him.

His face reddened and his eyes sparkled with electricity as he told her, "Actually Maeve, darling, I don't have to tell you anything. They'll be here soon," he laughed and told her, "and I can't control them. If I were you, I'd run, now while you can. Go," he commanded as spittle formed at the edges of his mouth. He began shaking and told her, "Save yourself and that octopus, if you can. I'm not sure there's much left to him, honestly. Or of me and forget your mother."

'Who dad, who'll come?" she asked him not wanting to leave him but almost frightened by his anger and what seemed like intense paranoia. He looked like her father but it wasn't the father she knew somehow. It was as if he'd been possessed by a madman. She picked the aquarium up and held it to her chest almost as a barrier as her father backed against the wall. He told Maeve, "You mother's the one you really need to watch out for," and in his frenzy he began to laugh and said, "She's joined the Shadows and as for me, well neither you nor the council can threaten me with anything worse than they'll do to me here. Plus, Abigor and I have bonded."

When she heard the last statement she found her mobility and screamed, loud and long, "WWHHAAAATT?" She took the aquarium towards him and pressed it against his chest to hold him to the wall. Holding him there, she closed her eyes, focusing on his mind, reading it, needing to understand. All she saw were these patients, the skinny people around them, coming from suffering the world over.

"How do you get here?" she asked them inside his mind.

They moved their mouths but no sound came forward. The vision showed them being taken from poor streets and neighborhoods all over, lured by money, work or love. Some had children in their arms. All shared a desperation so strong she was overcome with a deep repulsion. She backed away from her father and asked him, "Dad, Is that it? A slave ship?" she asked him. "How could you do anything like this? What did he do to you?" She hated Abigor in that moment and couldn't believe this was her father. Something had happened to him in the process when he reassembled, she reasoned. She watched him slide down the wall and drop to the floor, sitting there, face contorted, laughing cruelly.

"What can I do?" she asked herself and then her father, "How can I save you?" She so wanted to make him right. But he only continued his rhetoric, telling her, "Darling daughter, admit it. Or at least realize it. We're all slaves to something. These are the ones on the lower rung.

196

But you're a slave to," he thought before continuing, "what? Being good? Helping others?" he mocked her, "I mean, look at you. Why are you here and why are you risking your life? Not just for me or for your mother. You've an inflated sense of responsibility my sweet. Let it go. You can't save this world."

She heard his words and looked at his pitiful state. But he had taught her differently and she told him, firmly and clearly, "Yes, I can, dad. One step at a time." She stepped past him, put the aquarium on the table and took the lid off. "I'll save you in spite of yourself. I know the real you is in there." She wanted to shake him and pull the man she knew out from the cruel zombie he'd become. But she knew that wouldn't help. She had to figure out how it happened. How could he be so changed? So instead she asked, "What's the connection between these slaves and the octopus?"

"Brains," he laughed. "Use yours and figure it out," he said smugly. "I know you have a very good one. You take after me."

She walked toward one of the patients and asked the unconscious woman, "What are they doing to you?" In answer, the woman grimaced in pain. Maeve traced her hand along what looked like an IV line but was connected to headphones. The woman was strapped to the table, with her fists as clenched as her jaw. Around the back of the bed, she noticed the headphone lines from all the beds connected to speakers. Even the aquarium with the octopus had a connection.

"What are you telling them?" she asked rhetorically as

she took the headphones off one of the patients and put them on her head. Immediately she felt negativity and fear, so strong it nearly paralyzed her.

She pulled them off, not able to hear more and asked Victor who was still sitting on the floor, "You control them with negative thoughts? And fear? So simple. So clever. So horrible. But the octopus? What's the connection?"

He laughed proudly, "Don't you see? It works on everything," Bragging, he continued, "Look how it worked on me." So that was it, Maeve realized. Abigor had experimented on her father and now he was under his control. He continued, bragging, "Once you establish the right vibration for negativity and fear, throw in some self-loathing and hatred, you can control anyone. The recipe's not new. Look at the news, read your history with Nazis, Taliban, heck right here in our marketing programs to sell drugs. But our method is more direct and faster. And if we can work with octopus, with their 8 brains, it'll work on all species."

She couldn't believe how her father was obviously excited. She watched as he had to stop and swallow the ever increasing rabies-like foam that gathered at his mouth. Then he explained, "We can pump these vibrations into subway systems or put it behind television shows or in the trees in parks and jungles and control the masses not only of people but of all beings," he smiled cruelly and continued, "All at our beck and call because they feel badly about themselves." He laughed as he told her, "They'll kill each other if they think it'll make them feel better."

"That's horrible," Maeve said and she pulled the headphones off the patients, ripping their connections from the wall. They stirred to life as she released their restraints. They slowly sat and she commanded, "Follow me."

But they were confused and didn't move. She knew Captain Abigor would come soon. He must have finished cleaning the deck and certainly would want to brainwash her as well. Was that what he was trying to do in those visions? Call her so she could do his bidding? She dreaded meeting him again, not feeling up to the challenge alone. She needed some back up, she realized. So she lifted the octopus from his crate and ran for the door calling back to her father and the confused patients, "I promise. I'll be back for you. Dad, follow me if you can."

Her father merely watched her and yelled, "Save yourself. I believe I'm on the right side of this battle. But don't worry. I'll be lenient when I win. Not like you were with me. No worries, darling," he called after her.

"He never called me darling before," Maeve mumbled as she ran into the other room where dull people continued with their mundane duties, zombie-like, not noticing anything. "That was always a mom thing. Could Abigor have mixed their atoms in the regroup?"

With no time to ponder and looking for escape, the large open porthole in the stern caught her gaze and, with the octopus in her arms, she dove through it and into the sea. Knowing that, at least, she had removed the attachment from the Zephyr, she swam through the water like a mermaid and hoped the boat and its crew were back at the dock. Undulating with the waves, the octopus gently wrapped his tentacles around her waist, neck and arms using the suction cups that lined his limbs to hold on. With these amazing tentacles and their feelers around her, she felt at home in the sea and realized the octopus was connecting her with the ocean's energy.

Chapter 25

While they swam fluidly toward shore, she sent her clinging octopus friend positive healing thoughts. Just before they arrived, Chloé swam in front of them, signaling they were close. Maeve smiled and held the octopus tighter, continuing to send him thoughts of love and healing. Still lethargic and weak, each time she visualized something kind and good for him, he had a gentle surge of color, and she could feel his embrace become stronger.

"How long have they held you there?" she wondered to him softly as she slowed her speed and they approached the marina. And she also mused, "and how long have they held my parents to turn them against all they've ever believed." She was so confused. But she became more lucid the farther she went from the ship.

Coming to the surface like a harbor seal, she looked for Sarah's boat. KB's, "Don't draw attention to yourself," echoed in her mind. She saw them at the dock and kicked her feet in unison to move toward them with the octopus in her arms.

Hanging close to the dock, she whispered to Sarah, "Hey, we made it." She held the side of the boat hiding in the space between it and the dock.

"Thank God you're here," Sarah whispered and bent low to touch her shoulder. She touched the octopus too and said, "Who've you got?"

As she did so they both noticed his color stayed longer.

"We need to put him in something and figure out what he'll eat," Maeve explained in a near whisper. "They've nearly killed my octopus friend here. And I found my dad at least. They've mixed him up even more," she confided.

Vincent came to the side of the boat and spoke softly, "Thank goodness you're here. How'd it go?"

KB came behind him, dropped to his knees and wrapped his arms around Maeve. She felt better immediately now that she was among like minded people. He released her to touch the bump on her head and, smiling genuinely, said, "You've a golf ball sized bruise on your head. It looks sore. You need some ice."

"Thanks. And, yeah, ice would be good. But we need lots more. How long have you all been here?"

"Just arrived. Good work releasing us," Sarah commented as she passed some items over Maeve's head to have KB stow them below. "I have a crate we could fill so he can be in water. You can't stay in there forever."

"I have a wonderfully large aquarium at home," Vincent interrupted nervously. "We need to go. People are noticing us. We don't need that."

KB cautioned with a hand still on Maeve's shoulder, "The Zephyr racing back surrounded by birds has already drawn attention. If they see an octopus in the arms of a woman coming from the cold spring Atlantic it may cause trouble. You never know who'll show up with the authorities. I'd rather not deal with it."

"Understood," Maeve said but the octopus refused to

move from her. She moved deeper into the water, taking KB's hand in hers and said, "We definitely don't need a scene. I saw Victor. He's there. He's the one doing this. I think Abigor brainwashed him."

KB frowned, "You need a seed to plant brainwashing. He couldn't be all that different than he ever was."

"You didn't know him. He's a great man. Well, he was. The man I met back there was a bit of a monster," she confided as she noticed the security guard coming down the dock. She continued, "I'll tell you more later. You guys go and prepare that aquarium. I'll come along soon with this baby running. Octopus can spend about 30 minutes outside water. I can easily make it to the warehouse in less. Fill the tub as well, both with sea water. I can get in with him and we'll work him off me. He's only afraid but he's got me in a firm grip. And you guys better move," she moved her head towards the guard getting closer.

"Swim to that adjacent marsh area. It's not that far from there," Sarah told her. "Got it," Maeve agreed, squeezing KB's hand before releasing it.

Vincent cautioned, "Lay low. We'll see you shortly."

Samuel touched her shoulder before she submerged and said with a smile, "Good to see you, seriously. Did you see your mother at all?"

"Only my dad," Maeve frowned. "But he said she was there. Mumbled something about her working with that captain. But I know that can't be right," she confided before she dove under the adjacent boat to move away. Sarah overheard them as she checked the lines one last time before they left. She still had a strange feeling about Samuel. She couldn't shake it as she and Samuel walked nonchalantly toward KB and Vincent who pushed the full wheelbarrow past the guard toward the van. The gulls followed them overhead.

People barely noticed, all so caught up in their day to day as Maeve glided like a crocodile toward the shore and then swam along it looking for the least obvious place to cross the beach. The cormorants joined her on the pilgrimage, curious about the octopus. Chloé moved her webbed feet to overtake them and once she did, pulled at Maeve's hair with her beak.

Maeve pushed her head in Chloé's direction and whispered, "Nice to see you too."

She found the small marshy area Sarah had mentioned and used it for cover. They all waited at the water's edge for the right moment to leave. Maeve observed, "I'm not cold," and turned to ask her new companion, "Are you keeping me warm?" As she did, she noticed an ominous gray-black cloud coming in from the Atlantic. "I'm pretty sure that's coming for us," she said to her new friend and ever so slowly left the marshy shore with the cormorants following.

On all fours, she crouched and, seeing no one, bolted for the warehouse, a blur of legs, tentacles and water dodging the cars and obstacles in her path. Minutes later, she nervously pounded her fist on the door. Vincent opened it and she ran inside.

"We've got the tub full for you in the back," he called and stuck his head out to see they weren't being followed.

He noticed the storm cloud and said, "Oh dear," as he turned to see Chloé and company landing on the roof. "Thank God we're all here," he whispered nervously as the ominous darkness continued toward them. He bolted the door behind him.

Chapter 26

"You may not like it. Octopus like cold water," Vincent told her as she gingerly stepped into the tub.

Maeve smiled and said, "No worries, he's keeping me warm," as she lowered her body into the brine and felt the octopus loosen its grip. She asked, "Where'd this water come from? You've got seaweed and everything in here."

"Right from the sea, of course. We made a couple of trips with the van," KB mentioned. "I think your friend will like it. There are some minnows in there. Crabs too, so watch they don't bite you," he laughed and then said, "I'm hoping he may be hungry and recuperated enough to eat."

"Great." Maeve said flatly, "I'd rather not be bitten just now. My head's still throbbing."

"It's never too late for ice," Sarah said and handed her an ice pack.

Maeve sat back in the tub with the ice on her forehead and let the octopus relax into the water saying earnestly, "Thanks. Hey, one of you needs to check on the birds upstairs. That storm cloud coming is for us. I did more than break your attachment on that boat."

Vincent shook his head and walked out concerned.

KB asked from across the room, "What were they up to with this one?" referring to the octopus.

"Psychological studies. It's so crazy," Maeve said. "And my dad's in charge of it! At first I was so happy to find him but then horrified to learn what he was working on. And I think they re-assembled him incorrectly. He used terminology that only Charlotte ever called me. He wasn't at all like my father," she held back tears and changed the subject. "But I found out they've been testing negative thoughts and negative reinforcement to control and instill fear. They had all these recordings playing, on the humans anyway, I didn't see what they did with the octopus, just the results. The recordings were playing horrible stuff, negative hateful rhetoric," she stroked the octopus and finished, "It changed the people."

"Your brain gets good at what it does. Believing negative thought patterns brings you down." KB said. "Plus, sound waves enter your body and align, or in this case misalign, it."

"The people on the boat are taken from dire poverty, wars, conflicts all over," Maeve told him. "They keep them in check with this stuff and near starvation. It was dramatic to say the least. They're zombies. I listened a little and, honestly, wanted to vomit, then run and hide."

KB remembered Marissa and his son, left in exactly those circumstances when his friend Pablo'd been executed and he himself had been banished. The single woman and her baby left alone amid the revolution. He yearned to know if they were on that boat.

The octopus relaxed more into Maeve, allowing two of his tentacles to slip off her shoulder, his large body now resting on her belly. The weight felt good. KB didn't comment but after a moment told Maeve, "Speaking of zombies, I'm going to check on the two up on the roof while you rest awhile. I'll go up with Vincent." Before he could leave, she told him, "It wasn't my dad. It was like a weak evil version of him. I never saw Charlotte. Abigor's done something horrible with her, I know," her eyes pleaded with him and tears formed at the corners as she said, "We've got to go back."

"All in good time. Charlotte's a capable woman. Your father probably took the brunt of it. She's my mom too, remember? And I've been with her a few more years than you. So don't worry. We'll go back but now is not the moment."

He left her there with the amazing creature she'd brought home. Samuel knelt on the floor next to her and said, "He's right you know." He took her hand in his and told her, "We'll get to the bottom of it. But I'm fairly certain that your mother will be ok. She and Abigor actually have a special relationship. You'll see. She'll come out alright. Rest now," he told her and she slid deeper into the tub with the weight of the octopus comforting her. The ice pack eased her headache and the exhaustion from the day let her drift into sleep.

She woke feeling a chill and moved to pull a blanket over her but remembered she was in the tub, still in her wet suit. Startled and feeling around for the octopus, she sat up and found him at her feet pulling apart a crab.

"Hey," she said softly. "You look good. Your color's back."

She reached her hand to touch him and he extended a tentacle in response, gently wrapping it around her wrist and laying it on the inside with a point onto her palm. She felt his gratitude through the suction cup hand and said to him, "You are so welcome and don't worry, you'll be strong enough soon so we can take you home."

She smiled then shivered from being wet for so long. Her hands looked like prunes and she knew she needed to get out of the water. Sarah came in just as she was unsteadily standing and reached to help her, "You ok?" she asked Maeve.

"Yeah. Just getting my sea legs back," she said with a smile. "How are you?" "Concerned," Sarah said. "That cloud off shore is gaining strength and moving this way. I know it's Abigor. It has all the characteristics of a contrived storm. But the damage can be very real."

"How can we stop it?" Maeve asked.

"We can probably only weaken it. But we need to get started soon. And it's best if we do it at sea. Less damage. Think you can handle it?" Sarah asked, assessing Maeve's energy.

"Of course," she lied since she didn't see an alternative and only asked, "Do I have time to warm up?"

"Just. I'll get you some foul weather gear. We are going to need it," Sarah said, sounding concerned.

Maeve called after her as she stepped out of the tub, "I'll just keep the wet suit on. I'm sure I'll be back in the sea at some point." She gave the octopus a last touch explaining, "We'll take care of you once this is over. You don't need another storm in your life." He reached his tentacle toward her and Maeve took the amazing arm in her hand. "I'll be ok," she answered, "You will be too."

Chapter 27

Storm clouds galloped overhead as she strained to open the door against a heavy wind. The birds huddled in one corner and stuff was flying all over the roof from the gale.

"I'm sending them downstairs," Vincent called over the wind as he and Samuel herded them into the stairway. "Hold the door, will you?"

KB helped Maeve hold it against the wind as lightning surged in the rolling black clouds.

"Hey. What about us?" Mark called from the pigeon coop as a window fell from its hinge.

KB called back, "You'll be fine. A hit on the head may knock sense into you." Maeve scolded KB, "We can't leave them there like that. We're Lights, remember?" Remembering her father's sudden change she told him, "I don't want to end up like my dad." She moved against the wind and across the roof to where the two thugs were tied and undid the knot at their feet. They stretched their legs and put their hands toward her as if she would undo them. She chuckled and explained, "That's only so I don't have to carry you downstairs. Get up," as she helped the two struggle to stand. KB waited at the door, still of the opinion that they should weather the storm tied under the table. Samuel was helping Vincent downstairs with the birds.

Maeve pushed them from behind across the roof to the door and then reached to help KB hold the door when Kevin took the opportunity to run across the roof thinking he'd escape. The wind pushed him from behind and when he reached the side, it literally lifted him over the wall, carried him for a moment and then dropped him into the waiting marsh. Incredulous, Maeve pushed Mark inside against the howling wind but he somehow thought he could fly rather than fall like his cohort. He pushed back against her and circled a leg behind hers to set her off balance.

She grabbed him as she fell to the floor and threw him behind her head. Instead of landing as she'd planned the wind took him, supporting him as if it were a magic carpet for a second before it dropped him and he fell solidly on the floor. Maeve walked forcefully against the raging storm to grab him but he came to consciousness and kicked her with both feet pushing her back toward the door.

"I thought you used a cane,' she called to him, surprised he could resist so forcefully. She helped herself to stand as KB ran toward him and grabbed him by his shoulders to lift him off the floor, then spun him around to take the arms they'd tied behind him.

Once they were in, KB bolted the door and told Maeve, "That's not on us." Horrified, she said nothing. She'd thought they'd been dead long ago in the battle over the PCBs. But she hadn't witnessed it directly. Watching Kevin hang for that second before the plunge was shocking. But she didn't regret it. Nature had spoken. She ran past KB as he led Mark toward the flock of birds downstairs. Sarah was waiting with foul weather gear.

"Like I said, my wet suit will work best," Maeve smiled and shrugged, "Let's go."

"Hold up," KB interjected and pushed Mark to the

side as he ran in front of the women to inquire, "What's up?"

"We need to stop this storm. It will tear us up. That means we have to stop who's creating it," Maeve told him.

"Exactly,' he agreed. "So what's your plan?"

"We'll make a plan en-route," Sarah told him and they moved toward the door.

Samuel grabbed Maeve's arm and told her seriously, "This isn't your everyday hurricane. You know that, right?"

Before she could answer, Vincent told the group, "I'll go with."

Maeve cut him off, "One of us should stay behind and watch here. Try to keep that bastard from killing himself too," she tilted her head toward Mark who Samuel had tied to a pony on the merry-go-round. "But If we don't succeed, keep your head and all the animals' heads down," Maeve told him.

"Besides," KB added, "I'm ready and we should be off." Maeve and Sarah smiled and turned to go as he continued, "I won't lie, I'm afraid." He inhaled. "But I've been in a similar situation and I can guide you. Even if only to hold the boat steady."

Samuel floated behind them saying, "Vincent, can you manage here? They may need me."

Vincent nodded as the birds huddled around him and another piece fell from the shelter on the roof. "Go," he commanded, "We'll be fine here."

Maeve liked having KB and Samuel come. Sarah was wonderful but somehow, having male cohorts made her feel more at home, more confident. After all, she told herself, she'd worked for years with mainly male colleagues so it was no wonder. Too, she knew they'd be outnumbered as her mind reviewed the people on board. With her mentors there, she'd be better able to gather the strength to at least disable the storm and perhaps even help her dad back to normal. She also prayed to find Charlotte. But as she hugged Vincent reminded herself, "one step at a time."

"See you soon," he assured her.

KB called to him as they ran toward the marina, "Stay connected mentally, whatever you do. Don't stop believing."

"Never," said Vincent.

Leaving the car behind, they ran to the Zephyr. The sea rose around them while the engine sputtered to a start. You could barely hear it above the raging winds. Sarah pointed the bow into the waves and checked the gas once again. "Barely enough to get there," she thought as the boat surfed into valleys where the horizon disappeared. But she remembered there was an extra tank under the back seat. "We'll come back with that," she assured herself. Climbing the waves, she focused to guide the ship as it crested their mountainous height laboriously. At the top you could see the vast darkness of the ocean and the lightness of the sea foam playing across the tips.

KB shouted over the roar of the storm, "The ship's the eye of this storm. Once we get there, things will calm down and we can stop it. It's easy, relatively. We only need to break them apart."

"Them being the captain? And?" Samuel asked.

"We'll see," he said as Sarah pushed on the throttle and they inched forward.

Impatient and nervous, Maeve called, "I can't wait." She climbed to the railing and as she dove in, KB shouted, "Wait once you get there, you'll need our help."

Samuel called after her, "Trust him."

Surfacing, she rolled to her back and crested a wave shouting, "I'll wait at the stern. It's the easiest place to enter. Get a line ready." Before the waves could force her under, she descended to where the ocean was calmer.

Chapter 28

Even the fish were leaving the area, their instincts encouraging them. Maeve swam past an incredible yet panic-eyed bluefin tuna, a focused dogfish shark and a school of herring who paid no attention to her as they rushed for calmer waters. Behind them all she saw the hull of the ship and dolphin-kicked toward it.

Cresting for air, a wave hit her in the face, and she coughed. Her old fear of drowning returned suddenly and she started to panic. She felt the unpleasant and illogical dread and flailed in the waves. Suddenly, Abigor appeared to her once again, his curls undulating in the waves as he laughed. "You're mistaken about it all, little sister. But you can still join me and your mom. You left before I had time to explain." Disgust replaced fear and anger pushed her right through the illusion as she coached herself, "Eyes on the prize." She regained her composure as, mermaid-like, she submerged again and swam toward the ship. Like KB said, the sea was calm there. She was in the eye of the storm. She grabbed the railing and touched the ship. "Weird," she whispered to herself as she felt an unpleasant vibration on the hull. She pulled her hand away and easily swam to the stern in the now calm water. She found a line hanging over the side.

"Not too trim," she commented to herself superiorly, "That's what you get with slave labor." She chuckled as she extended it and noticed The Zephyr struggling outside the eye. She dove in and took the line to them, throwing it to KB

215

and yelling, "Tie this tightly and pull. Something wild's going on in there. The whole ship is vibrating."

KB secured the line and Maeve rode a wave onto the stern yelling over the storm, "Sarah keep going. You're almost there." Then she ran to help KB tug the line. He took her arm and told her seriously, "Good to see you."

"Likewise," she told him.

Then, as if passing a wall, they moved into the eye: peaceful and calm, blue sky overhead, storm clouds circling the perimeter.

"Incredible," Samuel said as they secured the Zephyr. They each pulled themself through the open porthole where Maeve had escaped earlier. Cautiously, they made their way through the hold.

"Where is everyone?" Sarah asked. "There's got to be people on board." "Unless he threw them over," Maeve said.

"I doubt that," KB instructed.

"Yes," Samuel agreed, "Keep moving forward."

They walked toward the helm slowly, expecting to be confronted at any moment, their footsteps echoing soggily on the metal floor. Each corner, each doorway promised an ambush. But nothing. Only a constant vibration echoed through the vacant space.

Finally, they arrived at the helm and stopped suddenly. About a hundred people were crowded into the open area, focused on Abigor who was in the center, floating about 1 meter above them all, his hands open at his side, face turned toward the sky. His eyes were open but rolled back into his skull with the storm reflecting in the white part that remained visible. The people around him were in the same posture. His face was contorted and angry, theirs showed fear and a level of distress that was uncomfortable to witness. Their eyes were wide open but, like Abigor's, had rolled back in their heads to show only the white of their eyeball. Their faces were all turned toward him and lifted to the storm.

"He's the storm. They're all energetically feeding him," KB said and explained in a near whisper, "It's the Shadows' strategy. That's what he's been keeping them for. Their fear and self-loathing allows him to create this monster of a storm and alter reality. We need to either change their focus or somehow break them free with positive thought patterns."

"Positive thoughts will take too long. The storm's growing. We need a break, a distraction," Sarah said.

Enraged by the injustice of it all, KB told her, "You want distraction?" and he angrily pulled a nearby electric cable from its connection. Sparks shot across the hull towards the captain yet he held his trance. But the slaves ran away, first from the sides and then from the center, panicking. A few remained connected but the calmness around the ship began to erode. The blue sky moved toward land and the storm reversed toward them.

As sparks flew, more slaves broke free of Abigor's hold and ran for cover as the waves intensified around the ship. Maeve moved to help them to the few lifeboats. KB continued to pull electric cables from the ship and disperse the diminishing crowd as he searched the crowd for his son and for Charlotte. Finally, the captain lost all support, and the storm came rolling back toward them. He couldn't hold it alone. Abigor descended to the surface and his eyes came back into focus. And he focused on KB.

Furiously, Abigor opened his hands to the electric currents shooting around the deck. They came toward him, like sparkling snakes and he absorbed them, glistening as the energy flowed into and around him. Revived by the new source of power, he floated toward KB calling with a deep otherworldly voice, "You? Again? Didn't you learn your lesson before?"

KB froze with fear. Maeve sensed it from the lifeboats where she was helping the slaves escape and called to Sarah for help. Samuel had floated to one corner searching lifeboats for Charlotte while he helped the starving and fearful crowds into them. Abigor was too fast. He manipulated the current toward KB and engulfed him in a paralyzing electric wave before anyone could reach him. He then walked slowly toward him. Sarah ran toward them but Abigor threw the current around her as well. Both grimaced in pain as the glistening shock waves moved over and into them.

Abigor continued towards them with a smile and said cruelly, "You think you can stop this? You tiny people, risking your lives for nothing." There was intent to kill in his now steel colored eyes. The ship heaved side to side as the storm's waves crested the sides and then retreated, splashing noisily as they looked for an exit. KB and Sarah hung like puppets in an electric cocoon.

Barely noticeable in the water and clutter that washed along the deck with the waves, a tentacle moved gracefully across the floor. Maeve saw it from afar as she ran toward Abigor who continued, ranting, "This will be the last time you bother me in this incarnation." He reached his electrically charged hand toward KB's throat.

But before he could touch him, the tentacle wrapped around Abigor's ankle and with a sudden jerk, pulled him to the floor, smashing his face and breaking the current. KB and Sarah dropped, lifeless, as a wave crested the deck and washed over them all. As it receded, the tentacle pulled Abigor into the water with it. He regained consciousness at the edge of the boat and opened his mouth to scream but was muffled by the sea that consumed him. At that moment, Maeve recognized an octopus' eye that surfaced on top of the foamy water.

"My friend," she whispered gratefully as the eye, with a mixture of kindness and vengeance, submerged and took his struggling prey to the depths. After just a moment the octopus stunned him with neurotoxin and then carried him peacefully to a cave deep in the ocean's bottom. As the storm continued above, the octopus worked in the calm below the surface to create a tomb of seashells around a lifeless Abigor, guaranteeing he would never return.

Chapter 29

KB and Sarah lay wet and unconscious on the floor. Without Abigor's influence, the slaves and even his officers became more lucid and aware of the danger. They no longer needed herding to the lifeboats but went on their own, some even helping others.

Maeve and Samuel ran to KB and Sarah. Maeve lifted KB's head to her lap as Sarah struggled to sit, asking, "Where did that octopus come from?"

As if on cue, a soaking wet yet smiling Vincent climbed from the hold and declared, "It was our friend. I've named him Ocho."

"I knew it," Maeve smiled. Vincent walked toward them and explained, "After you left, he was uneasy and wouldn't stay in the tub. He climbed along the floor and I caught him by the door. I knew he needed to get to the sea and to you, Maeve. Even though the storm was howling, he carried me all this way through the ocean. It was amazing," he paused and wiped the wet hair from his forehead as he declared, "I have a new idea for a carnival ride now." The ship let out a creaking groan. Although the people were recovering, the ship was not. "And apparently Ocho got us here just in time." Vincent commented.

Maeve helped KB to sit and told him, "Stay here for a moment. I'll be right back." Then she asked Vincent, "See how the Zephyr is, will you? It's tied to the stern." Ironically, as he turned to go, Maeve saw the Zephyr barreling toward land and recognized the passengers. Charlotte and Victor had commandeered the boat and now Charlotte was driving them toward the now calm shore. "What?" she cried incredulously.

"Seriously?" Samuel asked, floating to her side. "I've been looking all over for her and she's left me? I don't think so," he declared. As Maeve dove into the now calm water, he flew above it like a rocket saying, "You will not leave me, my darling Charlotte."

Simultaneously from the ocean and the sky, Maeve and Samuel descended on the Zephyr, Maeve at the bow while Samuel slowly descended into the stern. Charlotte pushed the throttle forward, determined to stay her course. Maeve merely muttered, "Mom? What's happened?"

As if answering her question, the Zephyr slowed and although Charlotte pushed the throttle forward to keep pace, it continued to lose speed. Samuel floated between her and Victor and with a grin commented, "Gas. You, my conniving Charlotte, are out of gas."

Exasperated, Charlotte pulled the throttle back, pushed the grinning Samuel away and told Maeve, "Well, it's not like I didn't want to see you. Honestly, darling, I did. It's just that you know how I like to avoid scandal and I'd been among those people all that time. It was grueling. And the sooner I'd get your dad out of there, the faster he'd come back to himself. A self I do love." She gazed toward Samuel as she said it and explained, "Regardless of how much I enjoy our time together Samuel. Why would that have to change?"

"Whooa. Wait a minute. You two are, what, lovers?"

She could barely say the word. "Samuel?" she didn't wait for an explanation and said, "Mom? Seriously? All this time with you playing happy home? And you were working with that monster? Abigor?" Maeve interrupted. "If we hadn't come, you'd have, what, stayed?"

"Not likely darling. But do you have any idea how difficult it was to reassemble? The council on our tails, blocking us. And then there was a mixup of a few cells of mine penetrating into your father and visa versa. I didn't mind, honestly kind of liked it. But he was so angry and so weak. Abigor took us in when no one else would. And you didn't seem capable at all. Honestly, it was time for you to step up. I had to let you learn these lessons, don't you see?"

Victor spoke up, "But then Abigor took advantage. He's not **my** son, so he didn't mind using me as a part of his diabolical experiment. So there I was, not at all like myself. Brainwashed, full of fear and self-loathing. The sooner I got away from that ship, the better for me. For all of us, actually"

"Except me," Samuel said sadly. "Charlotte, I came all this way for you."

Without regard that Victor was there, Charlotte said, "But Samuel, what's wrong with what we have?"

"It's just not enough anymore," Samuel sighed and began to levitate off the floor. "It's never been enough, honestly, and I'm done accepting less." He continued to float upward, into the sky. "I'll be in touch Maeve. But Charlotte, good bye. Victor, good luck."

Maeve reached for him but he floated quickly away. She swore she saw tears forming in his eyes. "Mom? We've got to have a long talk. Abigor's your son? My half-brother?" Signals from a relatively distant Coast Guard vessel interrupted her and they watched in horror as the Talisman started to take on water drastically.

"But now isn't the moment. We've got to go," she told them and, with a smirk on her face, reached under the dash to flip the switch to the second gas tank. Charlotte bit her lip, wishing she'd paid more attention.

"You could learn a thing or two by doing so," Maeve told her mom, having easily read her mind.

Charlotte shrugged the comment off and merely whispered, "I can get him back."

"I doubt that," Maeve commented as she started the engine and they raced back to the now half sunken ship telling her mother, "Why don't you just take care of what you have."

Chapter 30

Slaves frantically rowed the full lifeboats away from the sinking Talisman as the coast guard approached. Maeve maneuvered the Zephyr toward the listing hull and saw Vincent helping Sarah and KB toward the side. She heard cries from the seagulls that flew overhead as she approached and threw Vincent a line.

"The gulls went for help," Vincent called.

She smiled and told him, "Great work Vincent." The ship made another unearthly sound and shifted weight further toward the starboard side putting it dangerously close to the sea. "Don't tie that too tight. We've got to get out of here and it can't be too soon," she said as KB and Sarah limped with Vincent onto the Zephyr.

"We need to get away from this ship before it goes down," KB said to Maeve as he slowly lowered himself into the stern holding the railing firmly. He turned toward Charlotte and Victor and demanded, "How could you? And we'll lose all the evidence."

Maeve said, "No we won't. Give me a second," and she raced to the helm to take whatever plans or electronics were there.

"Leave it," Sarah called weakly after her. "The coast guard's coming. They can take it from here."

"We need to see it first," KB told her.

Incredulous but exhausted, Sarah could only shake her head. KB answered, "I promise we'll give it to them later."

"You can't do it all KB. At some point you need to trust," Sarah scolded him. "I trust. But trust me. We need to see that intel first. We'll get it to them after."

"He's right, you know," Charlotte told her.

"You've no room to say that," Sarah said and before Victor could open his mouth she spat, "Nor you. Stay still or I'll throw you off my boat with my bare hands."

The coast guard called from a bull horn to move people from the side of the boat. The slaves who didn't fit in the lifeboats panicked. A few who could swim, dove in and started swimming to the rescuers. KB weakly searched for any who even faintly resembled his son but, overwhelmed by the strain of his battle with Abigor, finally let go, closed his eyes and shook his head, not wanting to believe he'd lost another chance.

"You've done what you can for now, KB," Sarah told him. "You'll get another opportunity."

"You've no idea how this feels," he confided.

"Well, I know how loss feels," she told him. "It may be different but I can sympathize. And I know that there's always a chance."

KB sat on the floor, his head lowered but then he lifted it and told her, "Hey, thanks for coming to help me there, on the ship, when Abigor had me in that hold. You risked your life for me. I appreciate it."

Sliding down the side of the boat to sit next to him she laughed, "Well it didn't help much. Just another person to be rescued at the end."

"Don't do that. Don't minimize what you did just

because it didn't work. The intention was to save me, and I am saying thank you," he scolded.

"You're welcome KB. I value you and I know we'll do some great work together. I'll help you find that young man and his mother, if she's still alive. I know you're looking for them."

"You never stop reading minds do you," he commented. "Yeah, I'd hoped he was here on this boat. I doubt she's survived or that I'll have another chance. But perhaps that's it, right? Letting people find their own way. Charlotte's certainly got that one down."

Sarah reached for his hand and took it in hers, "Don't become like Charlotte. People don't need to fall. They need help to stand. From there, yeah, you can leave them alone but a helping hand goes a long way when you are down like these folk." She squeezed his hand and decided Charles may be right. Perhaps she could let someone in. Perhaps it was KB.

KB felt a surge of energy from Sarah's touch. But he'd silently held out hope of finding his family for so long. Now he believed his chance had disappeared.

Sarah understood and told him, "KB, you've done so much good. Let that one go." He shook his head in response but didn't release her hand.

Chapter 31

At the helm, Maeve flew through the open door and grabbed soggy plans that had scattered over the floor as well as those that were rolled next to the wheel. She took the few electronic items she could find. But when the ship groaned again and listed heavily toward its side, anything not fastened down slid away. She held the wheel for stability as she stuffed what she could into a plastic bag that had been floating on the floor. Then she pushed it all down the back of her wet suit before she ran to the stern and jumped into the Zephyr saying, "Let's go. This ship is going down and we don't want to be near it."

"Did you get all the papers and info?" KB asked in a weak yet determined voice.

"I got what I could," she told him and pushed the boat to cast off. Sarah tucked a buoyancy cushion under KB and behind his back so he could rest before she guided Charlotte and Victor to the stern seats telling them, "Stay here or I'll throw you over."

Charlotte started to argue but Victor told her, "Leave it Char. Or I'll help her."

Sarah inhaled deeply and pulled herself to the wheel, leaving space for Maeve to stand next to her as she turned to check on her motley crew and smiled, saying, "Hold on." Maeve put her hand over Sarah's to help push the throttle forward saying, "Let's get out of here."

Vincent left Maeve his seat and moved next to KB who closed his eyes and cloaked the Zephyr as they left the chaos behind them. The coast guard never even noticed them. Maeve stayed at the helm with Sarah but sat and extended her arm to the side to let her fingers playfully feel the wind and the odd splash of water rising from the hull. Then she ran her hand across her still bald head and smiled, feeling content with their victory. Sarah accelerated banking left toward Jamaica Bay and said, "Well done, Eco-woman. You've been initiated."

Maeve laughed heartily. Sarah swore she saw an electric spark in her green eyes as she answered, "Yes indeed. Eco-woman has."

ABOUT THE AUTHOR

Fanny Barry is an author, yogi, artist and engineer from Boston Massachusetts but who now shares her time between Tulum Mexico and Harrington Maine. Apart from her yoga practice, she finds creative inspiration in the people and natural places she seeks out on long walks alone or with four legged friends in both her homes. Her other works include; "I Wish I Knew, Notes from a Breast Cancer Survivor"; "Map of Life and Beauty", her memoir; and the first "Eco Woman, the Transformation". This is her second in the series but not the last as the world needs some saving yet.

Look for her at fannybarry.com and on social as fannybarry.

www.ingramcontent.com/pod-product-compliance
Lightning Source LLC
Chambersburg PA
CBHW031223260626
47169CB00007B/2174